INSIDE & OUT
by Jim Jackson

I0625167

H.M.PRISON
GREYWALL
Holtby, South Riding

Typeset by Jonathan Downes,
Edited: Corinna Downes
Proofed: Barry Payne
Cover and Layout by SPiderKaT for CFZ Communications
Using Microsoft Word 2000, Microsoft Publisher 2000,
Adobe Photoshop CS.

First published in Great Britain by CFZ Press

CFZ Press
Myrtle Cottage
Woolsery
Bideford
North Devon
EX39 5QR

ISBN: 978-1-909488-52-6

Special thanks to Nick Arnold, Barry Payne, Cyril Williams, Ross Collier, and other members of the Appledore Writer's Group for their encouragement and support.

C⊕NTENTS

KN⊕CKERS ⊕UT

There's no honour amongst thieves. That's what they say isn't it in the old well-worn cliché? And I am sure that from time to time you have had occasion to say much the same thing yourself. Which is, I fear, compelling evidence that either your notion of honour is sadly obsolescent or, as is more likely, that you have made the acquaintance of very few thieves on a social level. To be fair why should you know any villains at all, living as you do, a model life of unblemished probity and sterling rectitude?

However, and with your permission, I should like to correct your unfounded prejudices in this matter. Even if by so doing it lays me open to a small degree of personal criticism. We shall see.

Many, many years ago, under circumstances too painful to remember, much less relate, I had been caught red handed by a bright eyed and bushy tailed PC, and his pal - an equally bright eyed and bushy tailed - Alsatian called Wendy, members both of the Birmingham Constabulary, whose fellow guardians of the law subsequently turned up in huge numbers to be in on the kill, and cart me off for a longish, all expenses paid holiday courtesy of the British taxpayer.

Had I given them my true name, and had their fingerprint search been a little more assiduous, they would quickly have discovered that I had recently been seen about town keeping company with a stout and prosperous old lag called Knocker Norton who had wisely slipped out sideways with the loot, before the blow fell.

Had they associated his name with mine it would be all the excuse they would have needed at that time to secure a magistrate's warrant, followed by an early morning wake up call, and from Knocker's elegant house and his various lock-ups, they would have lifted enough hot goodies, such as compromising videos of vulnerable people in the public eye, used notes, and dodgy motorcars. Not to mention thermic lances, oxy-acetylene cutting gear, gelignite and architects' drawings of prominent financial institutions to have presaged a rounding up to perversely mirror the World War Two evacuation of kids to the countryside. So naturally I kept schtum, answered to the name of Jimmy Smith for three years, (might easily have been five) in Wakefield Trinity. Which is way, way ooop North. When on humanitarian grounds I should have served my whack in Brixton, or Wormwood Scrubs, perish the thought, discussing the shortage of Semtex and the virtues of short delay detonators with old chums, where my true identity would have quickly become known.

Knocker Norton, a gentleman of the old school of thievery, in acknowledgement of my forbearance, organised a coming out party to make history. At the Dorchester no less. Dusty Springfield sang for us in a private suite on the top floor and the personal chef of the Sultan of Brunei cooked fillet steak at my table. With a knife sharper than a razor he sliced smoked salmon paper thin and flambéed Crepes Suzette in vintage brandy. Good old Knocker had a Saville Row tailor run up several suits for me from measurements taken in the nick, and had a dozen silk shirts flown in from Balman in Paris. All of which would have been enough in itself, but May and June - centrefolds from 'Wrassle' magazine served the 'After Eight' mints in a most alluring and original way before disappearing with me to complete my homecoming in the master bedroom. God, no wonder I look old now.

All that was a few years back, but I am sure that you can imagine the obligation I felt myself to be under when I subsequently learned that Knocker had had his conviction for his part in the Muswell Hill Sorting Office blag declared unsafe by the Court of Appeal. It consequently fell to me as a duty of honour to organise something equally special.

The word which filtered out from Maidstone Prison Infirmary, where he had been under observation for angina, was that he didn't want any excitement. Just a quiet meal with a few friends followed by a night in the sack with Claire Rayner.

Yes! That Claire Rayner. I couldn't believe it either. It must be the side effect of some vile concoction they put into prison food to keep the beast in its stable. Well I ask you. He had two chances of that ever happening. A microscopic, electron sub-atomic-sized chance, and no chance whatsoever. Oh my giddy aunt. How was I going to be able to do right by Knocker as the code of honour in our community demanded? To make matters worse, his wife Nora, who had led her own life for years, was all for the idea. We had met in the tea room of Fortnam & Mason to discuss the party.

"Do him the world of good," she said pouring the Earl Grey with stylish elan. "Might be the last chance he gets to let his hair down. What there is of it." This last remark with a tinkling laugh.

Was it my imagination? Was it? I thought it was. But did a spark jump between our fingers as she passed the Scottish shortbread?

No. Yes.

No, no, no, certainly not. But still a chap can dream. Imagination has pathways Horatio, which we know not of. Quite a muffin was little Nora with her cute button of a nose and wild blond hair. But, phew. More than my life's worth to get involve ... question of honour don't you see. Not to mention the cost and social inconvenience of reconstructive surgery if Knocker ever found out. And there I sat fretting and stewing for the next couple of months wondering what to do for the best, whilst the fag end of another concurrent sentence ran its course for Knocker.

I was at a loss until one evening I bumped into Chancer Cusack in The Republican Club off the Kilburn High Road where he had been free-loading off of some American tourists with exciting stories about der troubles, der IRA and der UDF in the glens of Armagh. All eyewash of course; he had never been to Ireland in his life. His troubles started with the CID and ended with the NHS. Not that the yanks could tell the difference after a skin full of Guinness. Chancer was in a good mood. He told me that he had been drinking all day and had not put his hand in his pocket once. Which is quite a result by any standard, and couldn't wait to tell me who he had seen earlier that afternoon drinking in the saloon bar of the Exchange Telegraph Pub. I suggested the pope and then gave up when it wasn't the pope.

"Ruby Murray," says he.

Ruby Murray, you may recall, was a very attractive Irish singer of the 1950s.

"Ruby Murray — you daft old bat. How much have you had to drink? Ruby Murray died over twenty years ago."

She didn't have a happy life and was buried in a Torquay cemetery, if my memory serves me correctly. I mused for several seconds on the prospect of being buried, dead or alive in Torquay. But the cogs and pinions were slipping and crashing in my mind as I tried to sort the gears out, and to get my thoughts in order concerning this doppelganger.

You see, Knocker had a long standing soft spot for Ruby. In fact, he owned all her records, even some old '78s on brittle shellac, and might not go completely bananas when he found that Claire Rayner was not to be had and would not be there to welcome him home into her ample, maternal bosom.

I let Nora in on the scheme and left her to make the detailed arrangements, whilst on the appointed day Knocker's minder-cum-driver, Pipps Peterson, and I drove off in Knocker's new Jag to collect him at the prison gates just as the shifts were changing, and the screws were climbing into their tawdry and down at heel Ford Fiestas to go home to their tawdry wives in their down at heel council flats.

Comparing their lot to ours I said, turning to face Knocker, "Let's drink to British Justice," and made ready to open a bottle of Moet et Chandon.

"No," Knocker replied in an unusually subdued voice. "Thank you Jimbo, I'll wait."

Whether it was he'd wait for the Bollinger at home, or wait until he had quenched his pent up lust on the busty Social Worker he didn't say.

"Step on it, Pipps," he suddenly said in a more normal tone of voice, as if his time was precious, adding, "Or I'll have your pips."

"I can't wait. I can't wait," he kept repeating from the back seats as the black missile thundered off and whistled up the A20. Even as we sat in air conditioned, leather cushioned silence I could just see his lips moving. "I can't wait, I can't wait."

He was just like a little boy, anxious to get stuck into the jelly and evaporated milk at his birthday party tea. Which in a way I suppose he was. With a perfunctory peck on the cheek of his young wife, he pushed past her into the house where he stopped and stood stock still, surveying the welcoming committee assembled in the large and opulent living room.

It was all the usual suspects, one or two bent coppers and a famous trade unionist. A few old mates from Parkhurst and Wandsworth and half a dozen good time girls with no shame whatsoever. (One or two faces from the telly and about half a ton of smoked salmon, caviar, oysters by the gross, and a mountain of sausage rolls, pork pies and crisps for the plebs). In pride of place, an engraved Dartington Crystal bowl, full to overflowing with pickled eggs.

These were Knocker's particular favourite. How it must have pained him all those months locked up with not so much as a solitary egg to bless himself with. Dark, pickled eggs with raw onions smothered in English mustard was how he liked them best, but they gave him heartburn, or so he said. Nevertheless, he ate six in short order.

"Now," he said, pausing to wipe mustard off his chin with the back of his sleeve and picking up a glass of champagne from a huge silver tray resting between the wings of an enormous swan, carved from a block of solid ice.

"Where's my surprise?"

This statement surprised the two semi-naked black trollops got up as Egyptian slaves with huge ostrich feather fans, who honestly believed that they were to be his surprise present. No doubt they would surprise someone else presently.

"Where is she then?" he boomed, his voice rich in anticipation.

"Where is my luvvy - luvvy?" He looked around the assembled company as the room fell silent. Then, ever so quietly, music could be heard coming from the drawing room across the hall.

"Softly-Softly"

You had to strain your ears to catch it.

"Softly-Softly, - come-to-me"

Now louder - the volume had subtly increased.

"Touch-my-lips-so-tenderly."

It had his full attention now and like a hooked fish it began to pull him onwards.

"Softly-softly-turn the key - and open up my heart. Handle me with tenderness…..."

Quite loud now, we could hear all the words distinctly.

"…..and say you'll leave me never. In the warmth of your caress, our love will live for ever and ever."

The sweet soft Irish brogue hardly distorted at all by the fifty-year-old record and the forty-year-old 'Dansette' record player.

The door silently opened and there she stood - Ruby Murray to the life. The light behind her, a little plump and matronly perhaps, but none the worse for that. She wore a magnificently simple shamrock green silk gown which left her shoulders bare, and as she glided elegantly into the room you could see that the dress was slit from ankle to hips and to those of us with an eye for such things it was evident that she wore nothing underneath. My heart was racing. If I hadn't known that this was an over-the-hill, twenty quid-a-pop street-walker, I could have fancied her myself, but oh dear me no. I mean Kilburn! You would never know where she'd been.

"Welcome home, now aren't you going to give me a kiss yer big ijit."

The blood drained from Knocker's gnarled old face, he looked grey and about one hundred years old, but I knew that he was only about fifty. Then he flushed, turned bright pink. His jaw dropped then his hands dropped. One of which held a champagne flute which bounced as it hit the pale sand-coloured carpet, spilling its contents in a little tsunami of bubbles. A midnight blue vein pulsed at his temple. His eyes bulged out, like, like - well, like pickled eggs. Not a nice sight.

"Oh! Ruby," he said his voice thick with emotion. "I've waited such a long time. The others, Claire Rayner. Angela Rippon, Edwina Currie. They meant nothing to me. Just fantasies, that's all my darling. Just fantasies. You see I got so lonely in prison and it wouldn't have been right to even think of you that way, surrounded by – scum."

I must confess that his glance lingered just a little too long in my direction as he said that, but I felt that to remonstrate would, under the circumstances, be totally inappropriate. He seemed to be having a little trouble breathing now as he wrenched open his shirt at the neck crimping an immaculate silk tie which I hoped wouldn't crease. He stuck his tongue out as if it were standing in the way of his oxygen supply. I thought for a moment that it was about to fall out and land on the carpet next to the champagne glass and flap like a goldfish.

With an effort he regained his composure and turning to me said, "Well done, Jimbo. This is magnificent. This is perfect - this is just..."

He breathed in a huge lungful of air. She moved slowly towards him, closer and closer. With a great effort he licked his dry lips. "Oh my, oh, oh," he said. "My darling - they lied, they all lied to me. They told me you were ..."

Whether he actually said dead or we said it for him we shall never know, for in that moment Knocker Norton took a small pace forward and collapsed like a sack of old boots. And rolling over onto his back his felonious spirit left on its great journey to meet up in heaven with the genuine Ruby Murray, who as a reward for his lifelong devotion would surely put in a good word for him when he was called to give evidence before the greatest appeal court of them all.

When the ambulance had come and gone and the guests dispersed, I stayed behind to help tidy up, the biggest problem being the great ice swan which had started to melt. I got soaking wet and freezing cold man-handling it out through the French windows and down into the garden. So bitterly cold, in fact, that I had to stand in a hot shower for fifteen minutes before towelling off and climbing into a pair of Knocker's silk pyjamas and Knocker's cashmere dressing gown, but even then I was still shivering and needed something extra to warm my blood.

Who's telling this story, you or me? I can tell what you are thinking by the look on your faces. Silk pyjamas, champagne, oysters and a youngish bereaved rich widow who hadn't seen her husband in oh so long. Like I am the sort of opportunist who would take advantage. Well you are wrong see, all of you. We were attracted to each other it is true, but we observed the polite conventions and bridled our passion as respect demands. We waited until after the funeral and were married by special licence the next day.

It is what he would have wanted I am sure. Someone to look after little Nora, and take the burden off of her frail shoulders. Someone would have to look after the house and grounds, ensure that the Jag was properly serviced, pay Pipp Patterson's wages, see that those Swiss bankers didn't get up to any funny business with his safety deposit boxes, and his various numbered bank accounts. It's a chore but someone has to look after all these things.

After all, it's the honourable thing to do.

THE ABSENT FATHER

He, Bread Knife Baker, more respectfully known as Bread, said that it was the deep seated trauma associated with never knowing who his father was that induced his violent behaviour and initiated his nascent schizophrenia which was manifested by the demonic voices in his head that compelled him to lash out with dire consequences from time to time.

You will gather that I paraphrase these mitigating remarks, what he actually said being unprintable and almost unintelligible as they dragged him out of my cell with a large piece of Greasy Gregson's ear still clenched between his razor-sharp, fighting dentures. In fact, his assault on Greasy Gregson had nothing to do with his paternity whatsoever. We, that is everyone except the screws, knew that it was a simple punitive exercise conducted on behalf of the all-powerful Clarence Churchill, loan shark, tobacco baron, and king of the wing.

I told him. I told him repeatedly not to borrow from Mr Churchill. But he was adamant and just would not listen. Well he's even less likely to listen now that Bread Knife Baker has munched his lug-hole to a pulp. I only wish that he had chosen to spill Greasy Gregson's blood elsewhere, anywhere apart from my little cell. Blood spilt in anger has a special smell to it, and there was lots of it. Great gobs of it splattered everywhere as

Greasy struggled to get away. I never knew that the old boy had so much blood in him. Who said that? Lady MacBeth I think, or it might have been Ruth Ellis. Either way it ruined my reproduction Hogarth prints, and my much admired pin ups of Carol Vorderman.

Still it's an ill wind and I had my cell repainted, new bedding and other stuff, all of which makes a nice break in routine. The other advantage was that I was given a new cell mate. The very chap they roped in to repaint the walls. Quite a genius in his way. Somehow he managed to make the cream paint more buttery, and the institutional sludge green more spring-like. With a new light bulb, the old place looked homelier than home did sometimes.

My new partner in time, Clive Limpstone, was not your usual villain, not a paid up member of the union so to speak. In fact, he ought not to have been in here at all. By rights he should have been in some quiet, open prison with minimum security and allowed to wear his own clothes. The sort of place where they read the *Daily Telegraph* and tune in to Radio 4. There he could have rubbed shoulders with struck off doctors and unfrocked priests. Not to mention the dubious privilege of playing Tiddly Winks with disgraced Lib-Dem MPs who have played fast and loose with their small majorities.

Clive's crime, if you can call it such, was to break one law to comply with another. Now I ask you, is that fair? A chap tries to do his best by all concerned and ends up in this grey walled tomb of the unforgiven. After cocoa one night he told me his story and it's enough to make a strong man weep. A painter and decorator by trade, compelled by the recession to work at anything that came to hand or go hungry, he signed up as a meter reader with British Gas in Croydon. No, tell a lie it was Mitcham. Just for a few months, he told himself, until the economy picks up and he could return to his colourful profession. It being some consolation, no doubt, that his hero L. S. Lowry had also been a meter reader in his day.

It was with an optimistic and open heart he went from door to door through hail and rain, wind and sunshine. One bright late spring day he was working his way along a row of pre-fabs behind the sweet factory, the air thick with the scent of boiled sugar, and early swifts swooping after the flies who gathered in hope and expectation of the bounty promised by the rich, sickly, sticky smell.

His eyes lit up as a barefoot lady in a pink candlewick housecoat opened the door to number 88 Maud Terrace. The recognition was instant and mutual. They had sat together at school many years previously. He had had quite a crush on her as it happened, but kept it to himself. He was like that in those days, rather reserved and shy. The torch he had carried for a couple of decades still burned with a hot steady flame, one which had not been dimmed by the march of time. Which was ironic if you like, her having married an horologist, a watchmaker from Putney. Hers was a happy marriage, as far as he could judge, except for one small thing.

Er, how shall I put this? Suffice it to say that fluff was somehow clogging up the husband's clockwork. No sooner had the little cuckoo heralded twelve o'clock, then it was 6.30 once again and the working day was over for the crestfallen bird.

Before Clive had finished his Rich Tea biscuit and drained his cup, she was beside him on the sofa pouring her little heart out. Her tears quickly soaked through his nylon shirt and melted his grand old heart. Looking up at him with those wide, soft, moist hazel eyes, ruby lips all a-quiver, she hesitatingly whispered, not really knowing what to say or how to say it. Only one thing, she confided, stood in the way of her complete happiness. She softly mouthed the word.

Sorry. What was that? She repeated it amid a torrent of tears.

At first he thought that she had said that she wanted a brandy and was about to nip off to Vicky Wines in the High Street, when she snuggled closer, far closer to his ear than was strictly necessary, and repeated her request.

A baby. She desperately wanted a baby.

Would he?

Could he?

She really had no need to labour the point for they quickly did, with breathless enthusiasm and great gusto. So much gusto, in fact, that three gas bills later she gave birth to a splendid little chap they christened Bernard. Healthy, but deserving of a better name I would have thought, but then what do I know about babies?

So there he was, having delivered the goods as per prescription. Clive was eager to stay at the crease for a second innings. But his dreams of a felicitous encore were soon dashed.

Enough was enough, she was fulfilled and henceforth would be forever faithful to clockwork Cuthbert the cuckolded husband. All too aware that she had lit fires in his loins that raged beyond quenching, she did the decent thing, decent by her lights that is, and introduced him to a friend in a similar plight, that of maternity denied by cruel circumstance.

Denise, or Dennis as she liked to be called, stood 6ft tall and had legs like a Turkish wrestler. Standing between her and motherhood was her choice of partner, who although she did not have any fluff in her clockwork was by virtue of the lottery of nature deficient in the possession of the all too necessary pendulum.

Once again he scored a bullseye, and with his very first shot too. How his fame spread so quickly in those pre-internet days never ceases to amaze me. From Dorking to Dartford whole regiments of women were taking temperatures and consulting calendars, tea leaves, horoscopes and the I Ching before popping an invitation to tea in the post.

Over the following long, hot summer, having found his vocation, Clive warmed to his work and went at it with almost religious zeal. It was Clive Limpstone first and Jethro Tull second, although he never kept a proper score when, perhaps in retrospect, he should have. As August became September his summer of love faded and his autumn of mellow fruitfulness transmuted into a winter of discontent. A foretaste of the storm-blighted seasons which were to follow.

By some malicious quirk of fate, it was on April the first that the letters began to arrive from the inspectors of the Child Support Agency. Like an Apache war party, enforcement officers from Bromley, Lambeth, Wandsworth, Croydon and Southwark surrounded him with blood curdling cries and threats. They had the scent of him, and began to close in for the kill.

So it was with a firm will and a stout heart he began to claim benefit from any number of Social Security Offices south of the Thames in order to meet his obligations, pay for his good works and care for his numerous offspring.

How many offspring I hear you ask? About 100 that he knew of, and 37 probables, but mercifully only 29 had contacted the Child Support Agency.

The others remain guilty secrets to this day.

As you may imagine it all ended in tears. The CSA called in the

Old Bill, who brought in the Director of Public Prosecutions, who invited the Inland Revenue to the party for good measure. Not being a regular villain, he earned a curious sort of respect in here by having milked the system of fifty grand. Not that he managed to hold on to a penny of it.

Being a gifted painter also helped him become accepted in our cosmopolitan ranks. A dab hand with a paintbrush and a good sport he would always help the old lags finish off their models of dolls houses, Spitfires and Lancaster bombers. He also painted a very workmanlike portrait of our Mr Churchill as Nero, complete with Rolex wristwatch would you believe, and redecorated the Governor's cottage top to bottom.

One morning months later, I was leaving the Governor's office having had my privileges restored, feeling pretty pleased with myself, as internal enquiries had made no mention of my possible part in the missing 10lb tin of cocoa. Now if my co-conspirator had managed to lay his hands on about an equal quantity of sugar and margarine my end of the transaction might have been a pound of homemade chocolate. Not that I would have been daft enough to eat such muck, but it's something to trade with. In the corridor leading back to our landing, I stopped to exchange a word or two with Mr Harrison; an eager newbie with his ambitious eye on the chief screw's job one day, though still a bit green.

"Morning Mr Harrison. The Governor seems in a good mood. I will swear that he smiled at me just now. His missus must have left him or something like that."

"Haven't you heard James? He's going to become a father. As if looking after you bastards wasn't enough."

"Well I'll be buggered, Crab Apple Cora in the club. Wonders will never cease," I said, not without a degree of personal discomfort. Do you know what it's like to swallow a mint imperial and suppress a laugh at the same time? Take it from me, it is neither easy or pleasant, but I kept my composure.

"Left it rather late hasn't she?"

"Well I don't know Jimbo. Women's minds eh? You can't believe everything you hear of course, but she has been a different woman by all accounts ever since they changed the wallpaper in their bedroom. I say, do you think a spot of redecoration would lift the spirits of my Sonia? She has been rather moody lately. I don't know why. Only last week I brought her a new spin dryer and an electric kettle the week before that."

I could hazard a guess, but dare not say what I thought would work with his Sonia, a recent mail order import from Eastern Europe.

"Trouble is, Jimbo, I can't hang wallpaper straight to save my life. Now that cell mate of yours, Clive Limpstone, he's pretty handy at that sort of thing. If I cleared it with the boss do you think that he would come around to my house? I can't offer him as much as the governor did, but there will be a few beers and bit of tobacco in it for him if he's game. I will do the stripping before he arrives."

"Well I don't know, Mr Harrison."

"Come along James, er, Jimbo, you can talk the hind leg off a donkey if you put your mind to it. You tell him that I would be very grateful, if you know what I mean, and so would the missus. She'll feed him up while he's working. Yes, my Sonia will see that he never goes without sustenance."

Fighting hard to keep a level voice I replied, "Well in that case, Mr Harrison, I'm sure that Clive would be only too pleased to oblige. In fact, I know that he will rise to the challenge."

FESS UP

At this time of year when the clocks have gone back and the afternoons become increasingly dark, with Christmas just a few short weeks away it is easy to see how some people manage to catch religion whilst in prison. It's all right for you to laugh, sitting there watching Credo on television or listening to programmes about ethics on Radio 4. But what you should realise is that there are many different pressures, hopes, yearnings and undercurrents in here. For one thing the authorities are all for signs of conversion, and a convincing show of repentance, piety and contrition have been known to influence an early release on licence. Parole, probation or whatever, and we all pray to some sort of deity for that don't we? Although in these materialistic and cynical times it is perhaps less easy than it once was to grease the locks on the main gate in this way, but still some of the older lags persist in trying it on.

One such was Simon Bakewell. Simon was known as 'Sponge' to his fellow inmates from his opening greeting of "can I sponge a fag" and used to drive his cell mates, me included, potty by walking up and down at night in the small confines of our cell muttering to himself.

"Unless a man be born again, yeah. I got that one. John 3 verse 3. Easy. Knock and the door will be opened unto you. *Matthew*

7 verse 7. I am a prisoner of the Lord. Er um oh. Let me see, ah yes *Ephesions 4 verse 1*. Ooo I nearly forgot that one."

Whenever he had a visitor, which to be honest wasn't that often on account of his wife having moved in with a plumber from Plumstead, or was it a potter from Potters Bar? No I tell a lie; it was a dog breeder from Barking. I knew it was something like that. The mind plays tricks on you in here some times. Still she was happy enough by all accounts. I wish I could say the same for his little girl, and don't dare mention how she passes her time or the company she keeps. Get me, shock horror outrage from prisoner 42519 WJ-A wing. Even in here we have our standards, just not always the same as yours that's all.

Anyway suffice it to say that he had few callers and those he did have were met with the cheery greeting "I was in prison and you came to me! *Matthew 25 35*."

To the governor he said on one occasion, perhaps with more volume, emphasis and enthusiasm than he might have done. "HE" will open up the prison to them that are bound. *Isiah Chapter 61 verse 1*."

"Indeed he will Bakewell. Yes, indeed he will," replied the Governor with a tight lipped smile. "Just in time for the Olympic Games after the next one as far as you are concerned. That is if you behave yourself and say your prayers."

Other converts had just about as much luck, and there were lots of them. The very cross brotherhood of Islam in exile, seeking salvation through revenge and the sons of Vishnu who had about as much luck as the Bokor Baka grand wizard of Dambala Possession, complete with his ritual calabash.

Makes you wonder; do they really believe all this twaddle? Well some more than others perhaps. But they were not all as daft as

26

old Sponge walking about learning his lines and peppering each conversation with a suitable quote from scripture. Some of them demonstrated such a degree of sincerity that they even had an old hard boiled cynic like me believing that, once in a while, the crooked path we all trod could turn out to be a road to Damascus.

One such convert was Christopher Martin, 'The Martian' as he was known, for even before he saw the light it could be said of him, with some justification, that he was not of this world.

Strewth! The types you have to live with stuck in here would fill a book. Now there's a thought for a long winter's project. But what should I call it? *Fifty Shades of Grey* perhaps, that has a ring of truth about it.

I shall have to give that some thought. But do you know, I really believed that Martin had actually undergone some sort of profound religious experience. He stopped swearing, gave away his tobacco and flushed his collection of mucky photographs down the loo torn into a million little pieces. All of which persuaded me that he had indeed, in some inexplicable way, found a path to salvation in Jesus Christ, and good for him I say. He was coming to the end of a very long stretch for GBH and rape and before the winter was over he would be free to worship his god in Westminster Abbey just yards away from the biggest bunch of thieves, con men, cheats and ne'er-do-wells that ever waved an order paper, so he should feel right at home. When not praying for us all, he went about the prison offering aid and comfort to all and sundry. Even to Rasta Johnson's flock of black sheep on E Wing. I tried to warn him that nothing good would come of it. 'The bredderin havin deir own mysterious beliefs. Voodoo an curses an tings like dat dare', but he wouldn't listen, so off he went to offer the comfort of the word to the sick, and unction to those terminally so.

We had had a good Christmas that year, well about as good as it gets in here. Ho Ho Ho Merry Christmas. Just a half hour or so before lights out on Boxing Day he begins to cough and cough, the spasms rocking his thin sun-starved body until at length he coughed up a great clot of blood on the Snakes and Ladders board just after Paddy McFarlain had thrown a six, which would have won him the game and three Woodbines, but before he had had a chance to move his counter. He was not best pleased, but Mr Churchill, who owns all the games and rents them out, went ballistic.

You should have seen the look on his face. He would have extracted compensation there and then but the screw on duty pressed the panic button and they carted Martin off to the infirmary like a sack of wet spuds.

With indecent haste the word got out. The Martian had contracted TB and not just any old TB, but Gambian Tuberculosis. A strain particularly robust and resistant to penicillin.

"*Ex africa semper aliquid horrendum*" as Cato the elder might have said when he was cursing the Carthaginians to buggery.

"Well I did try and warn the silly old sod what he might expect, though I must confess it was the ill effects of an attack from a far larger pathogenic organism I had in mind. One with a teaspoon honed to near razor sharpness and a monomaniacal grievance going back a hundred years or so.

They lifted him out of the general ward double quick and gave him a nice little room in quarantine where, in spite of the protein rich diet, oxygen cylinder and increasingly massive shots of antibiotics in the Khyber, he began to fade away. It was whispered that it was only a matter of days, hours even, before he crossed over to collect on the insurance policy he had worked so hard upon these past few months. He must be well in credit with the Lord by now.

Like everyone else I expected him to snuff it, and ever the optimist, expected the routines on our wing to return to something like normality. What I did not expect was to be rousted out in the middle of a lovely dream and away from the loving embrace of Rosemary Clooney just as we were getting down to the good stuff.

Mr Richards was prodding me with no thought for my comfort or dignity, and Mr Royle - Oily Roylee our Chaplain - stood there looking grave. "He's slipping away Jimbo and he keeps calling for his brother in Christ."

"I didn't know he had a brother, and anyway I don't have his address. Can I go back to sleep now?"

"It's you he wants James," said Mr Richards with more prodding. "So get up and get your strides on like the reverend gentleman asks, cos I'm not asking, I'm telling." At which point he stops prodding and pulls my blankets off onto the floor.

At this juncture, Pick Feet Pete, my cell mate in the upper bunk, growls. "I say Jimbo, I would consider it a tremendous kindness if you would comply with their request and depart with some alacrity. It is rather inclement with that door wide open don't you know."

That is not exactly what he said. He used far fewer words to convey the self-same import and with far greater feeling, the Anglo Saxon elements of which made the Chaplain blush to his bootstraps.

"Quickly Jimbo, he's slipping away fast now and it would be the greatest comfort to him if some of his friends could be at his bedside, holding hands in silence to pray for the easy release of his soul."

I was about to say sod off, he's no friend of mine and please can I go back to sleep now. I was exhausted, sleeping badly as it was on account of being 100 Rothmans in debt to Mr Churchill. But I kept my mouth firmly shut and tried to look grimly earnest and caring. I mean, it can't hurt to build up a little credit with the good old C of E now can it? In my everyday shoes with the laces untied and no socks, I shuffled along to the hospital wing. Hells teeth, he looked dead already; his dentures out, arms as thin as mop handles and the skin of his face like a jaundiced scrotum.

"Ah Jimbo," he said in a croaking whisper. "So good of you to come. Will you kneel and pray for my deliverance good pilgrim that you are. I have looked into your dear soul you see." With this his rheumy old eyes rolled skyward. "Come, I can see you are shy before these people. Pay them no mind. Let us be fellows in Jesus this one last time."

Who did he think I was?

Knowing me as well as you do now you can believe that it took all my self-control not to say something about sex and travel, so like a good dutiful Christian I dropped down on my knees, and with bowed head clenched my hands.

Oily Roylee starts to beseech the Lord in a louder voice than was necessary, as if God were a bit deaf, as our man falls back upon his pillows open mouthed. This is it I thought, but after long seconds he rallied a little. "Father, he gasped, "I can feel the cold hand of death upon me. I want to, I need to, I must, confess my sins. Oh! How I have sinned and must confess before it's too late, and I stand naked before the throne of the lamb defenceless and ashamed of all my wickedness."

Ho ho! thinks I, this has to make up for all my inconvenience. All that rape and mayhem with perhaps just a dash of paedophilia thrown in for good measure. He must have been misbehaving himself for donkey's years.

"Perhaps we should be alone," says Oily Roylee looking at Mr Richards, the doctor and myself.

"No No! I want to confess my sins to the whole wide world; let them stay. Fetch the governor and I shall want a tape recorder and a bible of course."

I could see that the governor was none too pleased; he had his Marks & Spencer winceyette pyjamas on under his cardigan.

If I was expecting a long list of torrid sex crimes, I was to be disappointed. After swearing on the bible he steadied himself with a sip of water and began in a halting, breathless voice by telling us about a row over a greyhound some thirty years ago. "God forgive me for I shot him and buried his body deep beneath the roses in Peckham Rye Park. Then there was David Winters. He saw me kill his wife Rachael, so I had no choice, I had to kill him too. They thought that he had killed her in a fit of jealous rage, and filled with remorse threw himself off the balcony of their flat. Oh sweet Lord, why is it always sex and money? Money and sex. Why can't we simply share these, thy bounteous gifts?"

Why indeed? I echoed under my breath. I could do with snuggling up warm next to a bounteous gift just about now.

He paused for a whiff of oxygen which calmed his nerves somewhat.

"Peter Duke. Got that? Write that down. I hit him with a piece of lead pipe outside the *Kings Arms*. I can't remember exactly why. Then I hopped on a number 12 bus to Lambeth and chucked the pipe in the river. Then there was the lodger of old Mrs Winterson. She paid me to evict him from her flat. I dumped his body onto a goods train from a railway bridge during a thick fog. A black brother is serving life for that transgression. May he forgive me in his good grace, for we are all sinners and prisoners of our lusts and furies. The path is rocky and steep and narrow is the gate. Are you getting all of this down? Leave nothing out."

Fat chance of that with two prison officers scribbling away like crazy as the tape recorder ran silently on, consciously remembering everything whilst the Reverend Royle just stood there gaping like a dyspeptic herring.

He refreshed himself once again with water and oxygen and continued, "My pistol I hid in a plastic bag with a whole lot of other stuff on a shelf up a chimney in the back room of 142 Wallbutton Road, Brockley SE4. My journal is there too with details of all the others, and my building society pass book."

For long moments he was silent, then continued with renewed energy.

"Oh comrades how wonderful it is to be washed clean in the blood of the lamb."

"Tell us about the others. If you, please," said the governor soberly, and off he went again.

I was enthralled even though I had pins and needles in my legs and doubted that I would ever stand up again. As far as I can recall, there were eight men and four women dispatched well in advance of his own mortality to present his compliments to St Peter, the reception officer at those Pearly Gates. Would you believe it? I even knew one of his victims. Only a whore mind you, but bloody good value. Far too good to be snuffed out just like that. Well as granny said, *play in the gutter and get dirty.* She had had her life's chances like anyone else, and opting to sell yourself in the street is a very risky business one way or the other. Still it's a rotten shame for all that.

Closing his eyes, he said, "Pray, pray hard for me now my good brothers in Jesus for the hour of my judgement is upon me. See. Here he comes and I can feel his mighty hand closing lovingly about my black heart. Hallelujah I am redeemed."

And that with a whole lot of beseeching from Oily Roylee, not to mention a heartfelt Amen from your own correspondent he collapsed exhausted back upon his pillows. The young doctor sauntered over and placed a stethoscope upon his chest. "Still alive, but only just. It will not be long now. Why don't you nip off for a cup of tea and a sit down for a few minutes, Father? You must be drained."

Not a word for this poor brother in Christ you note so I just sat there like a lemon. The governor had gone off to his breakfast, leaving officer Richards to hover over me in case I stole a bed pan or something. I just closed my eyes and nodded off on an uncomfortable tubular chair.

It's a funny thing about dreams; you close your eyes and start to imagine all sorts of lovely things to do in the company of Rosemary Clooney, and the next thing you know you are misbehaving with big Sandra from the bacon counter in the Co-op, upstairs on a number 37 bus. Dear me, what that woman wanted to do to me don't bear repeating. There must be a message in there somewhere, but we were both disappointed because just then Mr Richards kicked the leg of my chair. "He's asking for you." My thoughts at this uncalled for interruption are also unrepeatable.

I had to bend over to catch his feeble words.

"Jimbo, be a pal, ask if I might have a cup of hot Bovril and a slice of toast, er with butter, not marg."

If I were honest, I would have to confess that when I bowed my head in prayer it was that this silly old bugger would pop off a bit sharpish so that I might go back to bed and my date with Rosemary.

Well the Lord had other ideas, and from that moment he starts to mend and within a week was back on the wing praising the Lord and all his mercies aye endure, for all he was worth. The fire of an enhanced faith flowed like molten steel in his veins and the expression on his face reflected the glow from the lamp of his enlightenment.

"Oh you sinners, take me as your mile-stone. For I have seen God face to face and my life is preserved, *Genesis 32-33*."

This to the assembled multitude in the queue for the mid-day meal. Beef curry as I recall; the rice so overcooked it was almost a solid. After I had eaten I was making my way back to finish my stint in the laundry, when I was plucked out and sent to see the governor.

Why? I hadn't the foggiest idea. I hadn't done anything just then to warrant such a pre-emptive summons. There was something of a party assembled in his office. The governor himself of course, Oily Roylee and Mr Richards, the doctor from the infirmary and Martin, with a wide beatific smile upon his grey old face. It could have been quite a reunion, but for two gate crashers in dark raincoats and size ten shoes who wasted no time once we were all assembled.

"Christopher Arbuthnot Martin before these independent witnesses and on tape, having previously sworn on the bible you were heard to confess to sundry illegal acts including multiple murder with premeditation and malice aforethought. Therefore, it is my duty to arrest you on the sample charge that you did wilfully murder David and Rachael Winters. I must therefore caution you that you need not say anything unless you wish to do so but anything you do say will be taken down in writing and may be given as evidence against you. Do you understand?"

Martin's ebullient spiritual aura faded away quicker than witnesses to a mugging, and his expression drained of blood assumed something of the bug-eyed surprise of a middle-aged rabbit informally introduced to Eddy Stobart on the M25 motorway.

For long seconds there was an uncomfortable and palpable stillness in the room. Officer Richards ran his fingers nervously over the handle of his baton and the Governor sucked his teeth, whilst I mused upon the messy but highly entertaining tapestry of human folly.

Christopher Arbuthnot Martin eventually broke the gravid silence with tear-glazed eyes and a trembling lower lip in the voice of one about to be flung into a thrice heated furnace for all eternity, and muttered in a low, barely audible voice. "Oh gawd what have I done?"

As the two burly coppers, one on each arm, led him away, he paused as he reached the door, and half turning his head fixed his pleading eyes directly upon mine saying, "Lord - Lord why has thou forsaken me?" Not that he or I could help him over much in that moment of course, but something of old Sponge's midnight ramblings all those years ago must have taken root in the sub-soil of my memory for without pausing to think I added.

"The Lord giveth and the Lord taketh away. *Job Chapter one verse twenty-one.*" To which Oily Roylee added, "Blessed be the name of the Lord. Amen."

C⊕UNT Y⊕UR BLESSINGS

Given the right frame of mind prison can be a tranquil place, spiritual even. A place to dive deeply into the soul's wellspring and emerge a new man.

A monastic enclave wherein leaden hours of boredom can be transmuted into golden insights of priceless introspection by the alchemy of penal incarceration. Over the past three years, for example, I have taken A levels in accountancy and politics, good grades too. Well I am in here this time for fraud and all three subjects go hand in hand wouldn't you say? Not much point in studying reflexology or any of that malarkey.

Having said that, I had a cell-mate Colin Cornwallis - who spent two years of a seven stretch on a chiropody course. I don't know about you but I can think of about ten million better things to look forward to than being corn cutter in residence in a place like this.

Oh! Excuse me. But it's making me feel queasy even thinking about all those thousands of stinking feet, black and white. Well more grey than white I suppose, that were destined to pass through his hands before they let him out into well-heeled suburbia. Even then they are never, ever going to allow him to go anywhere near little girls' tiny tootsies and toes, which of course landed him in here in the first place.

Nice little earner though I dare say. A ciggy here and there soon mounts up. Now that I think about it, it is little enterprises like that which make life just about tolerable for some of the mugs in here. Whenever someone mentions wheeling and dealing in the nick everyone thinks of tobacco barons, but that's just currency speculation, Old Holborn being the gold standard. But it's so much more than that. Apart from the obvious little services, protection, haircuts, letter writing and the old Oscar Wilde caper, if your taste runs to that sort of thing, then there is the hire of the various bits of lethal hardware that survival may require from time to time.

You name it, there is a specialist retailer on hand ready to sort you out, or somebody else should the need arise. You may take it as gospel that there are some very weird things going on, and not just on B Wing. I thought that I had heard it all when I learned of a couple of characters over there who had set up in competition to Elizabeth Arden. Ding-Dong. Avon Calling.

These boyos were turning out about a kilo of lipstick a week in half a dozen shades. Candle wax and cochineal mostly, cooked up after lights out in an enamel piss pot. Even the soot on the bottom of the pot ended up as mascara. The butch butterflies couldn't get enough of their products. Hair gel made from floor polish, and soap was a firm favourite as was nail varnish made from Tippex, if they could lift any from the governor's office. That was a luxury product on account of the short supply of the feedstock.

This little industry took, or so I thought, the HMP Award for enterprise, but a couple of months later I was to be proved wrong.

I was sitting one wet Saturday afternoon in the visitors' room listening to the rain hammering on the grimy windows as my aunt Pru went on and on about the never ending pageant of events in Camberwell's Nelson Road.

Mrs Dean's new lodger over at number 67. How the milkman had short changed old Mrs Stanwick. How the darkies were moving in everywhere and Oh! What a paradise on earth Camberwell Green had been before the war. I closed my eyes and could picture, with no effort at all, the smoky, hugger-mugger comfort of the saloon bar of the Tiger's Head, with a pint of best in one hand and a large gold watch in the other. Gold watch - that's Scotch to you. When I heard a voice behind me say:

"Will you do that for me Billy? Phone the Bishop and tell him it's urgent- you must tell him."

I missed the next bit behind one of Aunt Pru's hideous laughs.

"Don't let me down. It's important. Penny will give you the cash, 100 dollars for the bishop and say that she's to give you a tenner for your trouble. Now be a sport and cut along."

Ten quid was a useful sum back then, and I would bet that there was a very interesting story behind those remarks. I was not wrong.

The speaker was a middle-aged balding man on remand awaiting trial, who - by his upright bearing and what remained of grey neatly clipped hair - might have been an officer in the guards. I was nearly right there as I was to discover later in our acquaintance that he had been an officer with the Royal Army Service Corps, as it was back then, who on the eve of his demob offloaded a small fortune in codeine and motor oil to a car dealer in Stuttgart.

You may not know it, few people do, but codeine is just as addictive as heroin. Not a narcotic of choice, even in here, but the yank GIs and the Jerrys couldn't resist it. Well good luck to the both of 'em I say.

I was curious, but not over much, so I forgot all about it until a few weeks later, on the promise of an afternoon out on licence, I volunteered to repaint a cell at the end of our landing. That in itself was unusual but this cell was to have only one bed in it. A square of carpet and two or three bits of half decent furniture.

Who on earth?

This was luxury to rival that enjoyed by Mr Churchill who, as you will recall, is the top villain in here and never goes without his little comforts. Who on earth could it be for? There were the inevitable speculations, and of course the usual sweepstake. Who indeed, but none other than The Major, as I had come to call him from overhearing a part of a conversation with a likely lad, and instruction to bung a man of the cloth a hundred bucks for purposes undisclosed but undoubtedly less than pious. He was moving up from the landing below to his refurbished suite with his arms full of books, and with no small ceremony. The governor was there, the chaplain, the chief prison visitor, and the landing warder, Mr Soaper, his boots all aglow with Cherry Blossom brightness.

I was impressed, but not about to show it. Curious as hell, but I could bide my time. After all I was not about to go anywhere any time soon.

Over the following days and weeks, the pieces fell into place like a jigsaw puzzle. Major Donald Winstanley's first venture into crime had very nearly been his last. Had he been caught a day or two earlier he would have ended up in Colchester Barracks Detention Centre where everything is done at the double and a disproportionate amount of time spent in polishing the kitchen dustbins inside and out with wire wool and Brasso.

As it was, he was a civilian when he got caught, and after a lot of argy-bargy with the German Civil Police, ended up taking a long vacation here. Did he now feel like a proper criminal? I suppose so for he had worked out a proper scam this time and it was legal. Well as near as makes no difference.

A hundred bucks and a few phone calls, and before you can say Hail Mary, a certificate arrives by Federal Express confirming on crisp vellum that the bearer has been accredited as a duly ordained minister of First Church of the Holy Redemption, Albuquerque, New Mexico.

His request for a cell to himself, as his religion requires, was at first met with contempt and derision from the prison authorities. Well the Lord moves in mysterious ways.

Perhaps not as mysterious as all that. A further fifty green-backs to his bishop resulted in a letter from the very reverend Dr Luke Petty-Floyd to his senator, who in turn wrote to the Archbishop of Canterbury, who in his turn sent a little note to the Home Secretary, who then had his principle private secretary send a telex to the governor here and before you can say "Pick up thy bed and walk" that's exactly what happened, in a manner of speaking. For within hours of said telex burning up the wires, Earwig Edwards and I were busy painting a drab green-grey cell brilliant white and putting up shelves. The major, now a reverend, gets a new cell and I get a dollop of Dulux in the hair which I can't wash out.

Over the next few months I got to know the reverend quite well. It made quite a refreshing change to have someone to talk to using words having multiple syllables. We got along famously; he was never mean with the communion wine.

It was all a scam of course, but you already knew that didn't you? He even had a price list, which his new congregation accepted without demure. Blessings, confessions and prayers so much a go, crucifixes, letters of supplication and indulgences, not to mention little bottles of holy water, which were also on the list. He even performed a full marriage ceremony between a couple of Nancy boys which cost them 100 Marlborough apiece. His speciality though were letters of reference for the newly released. You had to admit that he had presence and the brand of old world charm which enabled him to put it over. He even counted Mr Churchill's arch rival Rasta Johnson among his congregation. A natural convert when he lifted a curse on one of his henchmen. True it was not with a black cockerel decapitated with a new axe by the light of a full moon, but a poor canary beheaded with nail scissors by the light of a 40-watt bulb, but it worked nevertheless. Mr Johnson was so amazed at the efficacy and speed with which this miracle was carried out he sent him over a pound of ganja, which he graciously accepted and turned over to Mr Churchill, wise lad. Word of the gift would have leaked out sooner or later, and whereas Mr Churchill was ill-disposed to meddle in matters supernatural, he would have come down hard on a potential rival in what he considered his own sphere of secular activity.

One afternoon just after lunch he surprised me with the strangest suggestion I had ever received.

"Jimbo," he said all serious. "How would you like to be a presbyter... you know, an elder of our little church?"

I knew what it was but could not for the life of me imagine why he had made the proposal. But as he had got me out of all sorts of fatigues on religious grounds I was in no position to refuse. Especially as I had just polished off a chalice of his best communion wine, and almost a whole tube of his blessed Pringles, so I nodded assent.

"Good boy Jimbo, I knew that you'd be game. That makes you and me for starters and holy Joe, the old lag who cleans my shoes and, get this, the Chaplain, old Oily Roylee. It's a godsend that he is even considering the request."

"What is all this about, Donald? You planning a bridge evening sometime soon?"

"Cards! Cards!" he said with feigned anger. "Cards are the devil's prayer book. Nothing so worldly or profane my son. Here let me top you up as you read this." I unfolded a dog-eared copy of the *Catholic Herald* with an item marked out in blue Biro, which I read out loud.

"A broadly based ecumenical conference of religious leaders is to be held in Rome this August. Smaller church bodies removed from the mainstream which have been under represented in the past will be made particularly welcome, a Vatican spokesman said today."

"O, Ho," I said. "And do you really think that they are going to let you out, just like that? Dream on Donald."

"No, not just like that old boy, but it has to be worth a couple of hundred bucks to dear old Bishop Petty-Floyd to fire off a suitably worded epistle to his Holiness the Pope to get his endorsement on our release. How can the old bugger say no? Half their blessed saints and martyrs found themselves banged up in chokey at some time or other. Saint Peter, or was it Saint Paul, even clobbered his guard, cut off his lug hole and went over the wall in a basket if my memory serves me correctly."

Pausing to nibble at a Pringle he continued. "Now just you think on it Jimbo. A bit of sunshine. Pasta carbonara, a few bottles of Chianti, some Grappa and real coffee. Real coffee old boy, not the cheap instant muck they dish up in here. Girls, Jimbo, girls.

43

About time we treated ourselves to a couple of girls. A nice little doxy in her prime for you and a rich, desperate old aristocrat for me. And who knows Jimbo, we might even be able to slip the leash and fiddle a couple of Vatican Diplomatic Passports."

I let out an involuntary Whooo! And think on it I did. I reasoned that even if the whole thing was a wash out and they laughed at us and said no-go we would have had something to dream about for a couple of months, and you never know they might just say yes and then it would be *Nunc Dimitus*, *Pax Vobiscum*, *quo vardis*, or whatever, my mind was on fire with thoughts of Moto Guzzi motorcycles and Italian women. I have always fancied both; "Cor Bless you Father," I said. "I'll drink to that" and raised my refilled goblet.

"Bless you my son," he replied, draining the last drops from the bottle. "And Amen."

Amen indeed.

JUDGES

You only have to look at them to realise that the arrogant old buggers really think that they are immortal, omnipotent and completely anonymous in their archaic wigs and gowns surrounded by the officers and artefacts, the paraphernalia and the panoply of the law. But some of us who come up before them aren't blinded by the trappings of office and some of us aren't as stupid as we look.

I am neither blind nor stupid and I have a pretty fair memory for faces, for I had seen this particular judge before. Without his wig, without his gown, without his spectacles and without his trousers.

Without a shadow of a doubt, as they are so fond of saying, our paths had crossed before and recently at that. By both historic tradition and by conscious design judges live a protected, repressed and cloistered life. They live, for the most part, a life in antiseptic, not to say sterile, isolation far removed from the rest of us, the great unwashed, the brutish herd, the hoi polloi yearning to be free. We are as but coal to a power station, empty bottles to a dairyman or muck to a farmer. Mere feedstock to that great leviathan mill - jurisprudence.

If we were to suddenly awake to consciousness like the tart in that painting, you know the one, having her soft bits grabbed by some be-whiskered cove seated at a piano, by Holman Hunt I think it was, and say "Oh dear me what have I been up to in my life thus far breaking the law on a fairly regular basis when it is so expensive and inconvenient and no fun anymore?" Do the powers that be then give themselves a pat on the back that their systems of social improvement have worked, shut a few prisons and retire a few old judges and in so doing save an awful lot of public money?

Never in a million years because as you will have noticed even though the legislature and judiciary are fairly dripping with senility. they ain't daft, in fact they do something rather clever. They turn a blind eye to certain offences such as vandalism, in particular graffiti, rowdy behaviour, criminal damage, littering and the like, secure in the knowledge that they have started a trend which is good for business. Their business that is. Having planted a seed in young and impressionable minds that the laws of decent public behaviour are something to be flouted at will, they reap, in a decade or so, the fruits of the harvest, ie: the poor mugs who keep them in the judge business. Great for the profession perhaps, but some of these old codgers don't have ten years left in them so they invent some new laws creating a whole new class of criminals that are easy to catch.

You know the sort of thing. Granny Williams lights up her pipe in the snug at the Dog and Duck and gets carted off to the jug for her trouble. Miss Tate, the music teacher, gets carried away with Johnny Jones, 6ft tall and 15 years old and is vilified when found out. It's a crime and Johnny Jones will be grateful for ever, randy not-so-little git. If this is a crime I can't see it myself. Only wish we had lessons like that in my day. There is no way that Johnny Jones is going to be made to feel like the victim of a crime. The law exists as it does because of all this equality nonsense.

If we want to bang up Mr Phillips, the maths teacher, for

making a slut of little Emily we also have to lock up Miss Tate, the music teacher, for making a man of little Johnny. Something not quite right there somewhere. I really must try and keep to the point, now where was I? I wandered off the point there a bit didn't I?

So there I was in the dock. Guts churning like a Servis Automatic, wishing for all it was worth praying that Justice Staveley didn't recognise me right away. The old excrescence adjusts his half glasses and leans forward, "Do I know you?" he asks. "I cannot try this case if we have met before. Your face seems rather familiar."

I, too, leaned forward and adjusted my glasses in a parody of his gesture which got a titter from the more wide awake persons present.

"Er yes," I said out loud, adjusting my glasses some more. You borrowed fifty quid off me at Catford dog track last Saturday, which you put on the number 6 dog "Sore Loser". You should have known it would come in last, I told you. Ask that blousy blond tart you were with; I'm sure she will remember. Now if you had only followed my tip, which was to cover yourself with an each way bet on "Destiny's Child" and ..."

He cut me short with a bang of his gavel. "Silence in court. Mr James, you will do your case no good at all if you carry on with this pantomime. Members of the jury, in the interest of justice I instruct you to disregard these remarks. The defendant has yet to enter a plea, and for the record I have never been to Harringay dog track in my life."

"He said Catford me-lud," said the clerk.

"Yes, yes, never mind. Press on. Read the charges."

It was then, as the charges were being read, "Handling stolen goods Contrary to Section 22 /1 of the 1968 Theft Act,", that I rediscovered my belief in telepathy.

If perchance you had planted a microphone in the old boy's head you might have heard him talking to himself thus:- "Impertinent, foolish fellow to address me in such an impudent fashion. Did he think he was being funny and wished to soften the jury? Bah! Men in my position do not go dog racing. Not sure where Catford is exactly. South London somewhere I believe. Anyway on Saturday I was at Penelope Throgmorton's delightful establishment in Knightsbridge. Ah! Angela, Diana, Lulu and Pixi. Was she really only thirteen? So hard to tell these days. Young certainly. So impish, so naughty, so coy. Oh my little sprite, dear little Pixi. Destiny's Child she had called herself."

It was at this exact point that his mental processes changed from electro-chemical to mechanical and became a maelstrom of bruised and splintered metal as the cogs in his head crashed from third gear to reverse in a matter of a split second. A great spanner in the form of the man in the dock fell into the whirring interstices. That fellow there in the dock with his hands in his pockets, standing there as bold as brass in his Aquascutum sports jacket, he had used those very words. He had said Destiny's Child. It had to be a coincidence, but no, oh, I thought his face was familiar. What on earth should I do now? Stop the trial? Order a retrial. Whatever I do he has me. Oh god. If only she had not looked so much like little Amelia. How Pater had thrashed me that time. Little Pixi is not nearly so harsh."

Now I really must digress at this point. No choice. The problem of having a little education and a bit of a reputation is that every villain on the manor comes to you with his daft ideas. Mostly rubbish of course, but now and again a right little earner. Do you know Toupee Thompson? No. Just as well, for you that is.

Toupee didn't need my advice, but as an undischarged bankrupt he needed a name to go on the paperwork at Companies House for his new venture.

"The Manfred Conference Centre."

I was on the point of saying no when he slaps a grand down on the bar of the Heritage Club in Bermondsey, offers me the drinks concession and five percent of the nett. So over a large G&T I became a director of the Manfred Conference Centre. The MCC, as those in on the secret will confirm, is a fiendishly clever cover for the most discrete, luxurious and expensive knocking-shop in the whole UK. Perhaps Europe. Perhaps even the world. Anyone overhearing MCC, or seeing it in an important man's diary, is going to assume that it was some cricketing thing. But we know different.

It was harder to get into the MCC than Whites, the Brigade of Guards, or the Athenaeum. Gad sir they even let women in there now. Country's gorn to the dogs what? With a term at Rugby costing an ambitious parent about three and a half grand, the annual fee of the MCC is a bargain. It all looked so kosher. Liveried doorman with *Debrett's* and *Who's Who* on hand in the porter's lodge.

Excellent kitchen, extensive cellar. Valet service for your Bentley should the ashtrays be a bit full. A cinema and a sauna. There was the Sybaritic Suite, the Byron Suite complete with all the whips, canes, and chains you could wish for, and the Schoolroom with suitably-sized desks, and a rocking horse. There were other rooms of course, but these were the main ones popular with the judiciary. All the dollymops and rent boys came in by taxi from Pinner and Purley, no expense spared, via the rear entrance of course. In fact, everything was on offer that an old Etonian could dream of. The fees were just a part of the income stream. By far the greater source of revenue was generated from the tapes, films and overheard conversations recorded, and kept on the master computer.

Some of these things were priceless gems. Surprisingly very little involved blackmail, the reason being that the source of the material would be instantly known, and mistrust would spread like wildfire. But some of these old boys just couldn't resist talking shop, even when having their arse caned by some teenage strumpet young enough to be their granddaughter. Big city takeover details, government contracts, and peace deals between countries at loggerheads would frequently end up on the computer and permit a wise investor to make a killing.

These thoughts, or others of a not dissimilar lineage, burned like a night-watchman's coke brazier behind the judge's old eyes. When you think about it, what businessman would not want an MP or a judge in his pocket, and Toupee Thompson had them by the dozen. We often joked about how many more tame MPs he would need to swing a vote to declare war on the USA.

Oh, he recognised me all right. I was the pleb who served him and Pixi champagne cocktails and peach Bellinis on Saturday when I was not at the dog track either. He was in a bit of a cleft stick. It would not look good if he let me off on some thin technicality. If it was too thin, he could be seen as perverting the course of justice and face court in his own right. If he sent me down there was every chance that I would grass him up to the tabloid press. I wouldn't of course. I dare not. Don't forget that I owned part of the business which would be ruined by disclosure, and even before the ink was dry on the newsprint, Toupee would find himself being fed to the pigs on some remote estate and I would be lucky not to be the second course.

The gearbox in the old boy's head ground to a halt and the face under the wig turned a sort of pinkish grey, if you can imagine such a shade. His wig shifted in a quasi-comical sort of a way as a hush fell over the courtroom. He begins to cough and gurgle. His dentures popped out onto the clerk's desk below, and broke the spell of timelessness. The clerk stands up, the ushers run about and the police on duty babble into radios.

No doubt with final thoughts of short, baby doll nightgowns, and fluffy pink slippers he stared with bulging eyes and purple lips into the great beyond as celestial sirens and flashing blue lights carried him away on the first leg of a journey to that great court of appeal in the sky. I wonder if he had the audacity to conduct his own defence.

When next I appeared in court it was before a Nigerian judge who would never have been allowed over the welcome mat of the MCC. Toupee came up trumps with a top flight barrister who did his best for me. Two years less time served suspended for two years and I was free to go. The irony of the thing is that said judge, no longer with us, had forgotten where he had left his gold Cartier wrist watch and reported it lost or stolen. It subsequently fell out of Pixi's pocket whilst we were playing a different sort of game, one not involving whippy canes or thrashings of any sort. I gave her fifty quid for it and offered it to a fence called Bruce Vosper who, unbeknown to me, had previously cut a deal with Chief Inspector 'Dicky Bird' Wren of M-Division and I, and no doubt many other customers were to be his get out of jail free card.

How was I to know that the ugly little woman behind the counter of his Peckham shop was Temporary Detective Constable Jennifer Pike? She certainly looked like she belonged in a pawn shop. Once again I found myself behind grey walls like I had never been gone. Fortunately for Vosper he sold up a bit smartish, and took the high road for the hills and glens where he now sports a beard and a kilt. Well, he better have his claymore with him if I catch up with him on one dark night, or his neeps will be in tatters, and that is a promise.

THE L⊕NG ARⅢ ⊕F THE LAWLESS

During free association some months back, as the other lags mooched aimlessly about the yard, Mohamed and I sat on the grimy laundry steps watching the flies and bluebottles practice circuits and landings on the large galvanised dustbins by the back door next to the kitchen, all under the watchful eye of Mr Whitworth who, as his name might imply, is the leading screw in this establishment. Mr Whitworth blew his whistle to remind us that only five minutes remained for exercise and as we stood up our conversation drifted in a roundabout sort of way into the morals and ethics of caste systems, which sooner or later will, without exception, stratify almost any formal or informal society you may care to think of, be it the meanest little Indian hamlet or the singing groves of academe.

It was, we concluded, no less true of the criminal underworld, both within and without these grey, beetling walls which symbolise society's displeasure at our cavalier disregard of its mores, conventions and laws.

"More's the pity," said Mohamed with a rare spark of punning wit as we were herded back inside. Well it looked like rain anyway.

You have all heard of the pecking order prevailing in the nick. The dark mirror image of society at large, which it contemplates as it bends to wash its hands of us and our little peccadilloes.

Famous billionaire fraudsters with well-connected friends, at or near the top and paedophiles at the bottom - er, so to speak. In or out, the graduations of the British class system are as multi-layered as flaky pastry. However, to a suave, velvet-gloved, iron-fisted, pragmatic manager of men such as Mr Churchill – remember him? He got me a job in the prison library once. Remind me to tell you about it some time. To him and his ilk there are only two sorts of criminals.

First you have your professional people whose only form of income is derived from the close study, pursuit and practice of crime. Professional, perhaps, but this does not vouchsafe any particular level of skill. For here, as in any other vocation there are the slapdash, lazy, incompetent, ill-prepared and just plain unlucky. Were it otherwise the prisons would be half empty. Nutters and perverts aside, the prison population is chiefly composed of such people, and by and large, people fit in where they best belong. At the apex of his hierarchy you will find a peer group echelon, which, in a sense, is analogous to the Law Lords, which in some respects it echoes. As equally powerful and reclusive, these men are at the very peak of the profession.

Over a dry sherry or two in chambers, the elements of a final appeal are dissected and discussed. The closing remarks of council, the summing up, the *orbiter dicta* and the *ratio decidendi* are microscopically examined, and punishment ratified, or not as the case may be. Ten years here. Twenty years there, or a well-deserved life-time tariff. Cold as these decisions are they are not awarded without a sigh at the vacuity and persistence of human sinfulness in all its many and diverse forms as the ever turning stones of jurisprudence drive resolutely onwards.

With the self-same sigh, and with an eye to the all too necessary expediency, Mr Churchill, or one of his elevated fraternity, may drain the last drops of whatever illicit spirit they may have on hand at the moment before giving a silent nod, which sets in train wheels, which perhaps may result in a punitive beating, a cutting, a kneecapping or the breaking of long bones or, if the transgression is serious but not venal, some impromptu and unwelcome dental rearrangement.

In the second group fall what I would call accidental or administrative criminals. These are, for the most part, normal, hardworking, happy frugal people. Common folk criminalised by the heartless stroke of the legislative biro. Usually no one has been hurt, no property damaged or taken. No insults hurled or blows struck, but in the eyes of the machinery of state, law breakers nevertheless and treated just the same as real criminals. Some bureaucratic form ignored. A little extra alcohol in the bloodstream at an inopportune moment. A reluctance to part with grandad's WW2 trophy pistol. Unpaid, unfair fines or the belief that hard-earned cash would be better employed on a family holiday than generous subsidies in the guise of overseas aid to African dictators. It is not unreasonable to maintain that our taxes are not intended for such a purpose and refuse to cough up.

We all cross the line of strict compliance from time to time.

If the administration employs people to make changes to the law and add new ones, it is inevitable that they are going to get broken from ignorance if nothing else. Having said that you have to be pretty blatant to end up in chokey smelling your armpits and wondering what unpleasantness awaits just around the corner.

If we are honest, any one of us could end up stargazing behind bars in some place like HMP Follywood. As you may know from the news, or a *Panorama* programme, Follywood is a low security prison; all struck off doctors, motorists, MPs and disgraced clergymen. There are bars on the windows, of course, but these are more symbolic than effective. Still to a schoolmaster with a taste for gentle - but illicit - romance or a businessman determined to keep the chancellor's greedy profligate fingers off his hard earned cash, it must seem like the oubliette of perdition, particularly when the gate clangs shut behind you for the first time. But to an old pro it's like a Butlin's Holiday Camp.

By all that's fair I shouldn't be locked up in here at all. By rights I should be quietly going potty in Wormwood Scrubs, with another three still to run. But you see I have had a monster slice of raw, fresh, organic good luck, resulting, would you believe, from questions in the House no less, order, order. Prison overcrowding, ya, ya, ya blah, blah blah and hey presto a few non-threatening, quiet prisoners, such as myself, are loaded into a coach to serve out the remainder of our tariff here in the lovely Hampshire countryside, or - as in my case - the successful outcome of an appeal whichever came first.

I was lucky with my room mates too. There was Kevin, an articulate and gifted medic who ran a most successful gynaecological practice in spite of having never spent a day in medical school, and Mohamed who was dragged out of bed one November morning for no better reason than that wife number three was the fourteen-year-old runaway daughter of Edwin Coats. Oh yes. That Edwin Coats, you must know of him. Merchant banker, Labour Party fund-raiser, Freemason and friend of half the senior cops in the South East.

Then there was Jacob. Lost a finger getting a small packet of diamonds out of war ravished Dongbia only to be arrested for a completely unrelated matter, and the stones confiscated by Customs and Excise as he walked through Heathrow. Now that is not fair, is it? As my very excellent barrister, Mr Jeremiah Cox, will tell you, as he has told the court on many occasions, I am a man who yearns to go straight, but whose plans are invariably frustrated by bad luck and bad company.

My crime and subsequent arrest and imprisonment resulted from no more than an error of business judgement during a carefree game of golf, on a crisp bright autumn afternoon. I don't play golf much these days, and in here of course not at all, for what had once been the sport of preference for Lloyds names and other such well-heeled high rollers had degraded over a decade or so into a pastime for oiks and plebs, scrap metal traders, bookies, chip shop owners and the like. The sort of people I can meet in any Old Kent Road boozer any old day of the week without having to lay out a stiff membership fee for the privilege.

Being at a loose end, I accepted Whistler Watson's invitation to join him, his accountant and his accountant's chum, Daniel, for a round on a course down in Surrey. Whistler and I go back a long way, remind me to tell you of the Kipper caper some time. Friend Daniel turned out to be a softly-spoken middle-aged sort who turned up in a newish Jaguar with a very posh set of kit. We all put one hundred pounds in the kitty. Winner takes all.

Need I say that I was five holes down by the 9th, and my wallet was building up for a fond farewell to my cash. Whistler, looking rather crestfallen and hard up since his last little holiday, suggested that it was time for a small joint so we duly lit up much as you might do yourself when under pressure.

"Is that what I think it is?" says Daniel.

"Red Leb," says I. "Naught but the best."

"Er, can you get me some?" he says bold as brass.

"Sure, how much do you want - half a ton any good to you?" A stupid thing to say, but it relaxes you don't it and you drop your guard. Quite clearly I didn't have half a ton of it or anything like it. It was just a joke. A silly off-hand throw away, Saturday afternoon joke.

Whistler's accountant clearly didn't want to become even remotely involved and wandered off looking for stray balls in the long grass safely out of earshot.

I agreed to get him half an ounce and we settled up in the quiet saloon bar of the Jackdaw pub on the way home. And that should have been that. A little favour for a friend of a friend, but against all the odds he kept coming back for more; never less than an ounce and sometimes three or four. This was starting to get serious and I had to change my supplier if I was to stand any chance of making a small profit for myself. Otherwise I was just his runner and the one to get into hot water if I were ever caught with it in my possession. Sometimes he would invite me to sample the merchandise as we sat in his Jag with Radio 3 playing softly in the background. Halcyon days what?

One afternoon he spots me in Waitrose, and pulls me to one side by the Cream Crackers and whispers "It's on."

"What's on? What's on what?" I answer, mystified.

Something on television you have an interest in?"

"No. The deal, half a ton. Can you still get it?"

The penny dropped. I did say that I could didn't I? I could have bitten my tongue off. I didn't have half a ton or even knew who had, but keen not to lose face I nodded, smiled a conspiratorial smile and said I would be in touch. Doing sums in my head I walked out into the Gloucester Road heading for Earls Court, and completely forgot all about the runner beans and new potatoes I had intended to buy. If I might explain my problem. I was not in the drugs business. It is a game too full of crooks for my liking. Mostly foreigners who are too quick to anger and respond with sharpened steel if things do not go their way. It was one thing to buy the stuff retail from Spiky Mikey, the urban spaceman, behind the sheds on the retail park, and quite another to have any truck whatsoever with the "bredrin" down on the front line, as Electric Avenue is known locally.

If a stockbroker, or for that matter a bookie, stumbles over a gamble which is too big for him to handle from his own resources, he will pass it on to a bigger firm in return for a cut, a finder's fee so to speak. It's the same in any game. In my sector of the grey economy that invariably means talking to Mr Churchill.

When someone of his standing is put away for a spell there arises more plots and ploys to assume the mantle of authority than Niccolò Machiavelli ever dreamed of, or Shakespeare imagined. I will not say that Seth Hardcastle had any official sanction from Mr Churchill to take on the role of heir presumptive, but Harry Mills lost interest in the vacancy when they took him to see and hear Dougie Foster try to first talk, and then swim his way out of the concrete foundations of the latest mercantile tower in Docklands as the wet slurry poured down upon his head.

Although Seth Hardcastle now lived in Mr Churchill's house, drove his many cars, and looked after his many girls, he did not have Mr Churchill's style. His doorkeepers, one does not say minders any more, had about as much finesse as a falling smokestack, and no doubt landed with a considerably equivalent impact should they have occasion to pay someone a visit. Ugly Jack Slack was, as you correctly suppose, as ugly as sin with his small gargoyle head and squat, deformed body builder's body.

His left hand was replaced by a steel hook. I am not sure which one was the more frightening, him or Fingers Finch. Criminals are sometimes called 'Fingers' if they exhibit some special skill in picking pockets or have the necessary sensitivity to feel their way into a safe but no; it was simply that Fingers collected fingers, just as you might collect stamps or beer mats.

He had, or at any rate said that he had, over one hundred in his collection. You may care to doubt his word, but I would not advise it. From my first approach to Seth Hardcastle it became his project, and if I ended up making anything out of the deal that was my good luck and if I still had all my fingers to count the commission I had not got, then that was a bonus.

I kept well out of the way as he set the terms, provided the transport, financed the purchase from the nigs' - er middlemen - and somehow managed to be buying drinks in his home town of Bradford's most popular pub when the transaction took place, but I could not escape being there in person under the evil eye of Fingers Finch parked inconspicuously 50 yards away from the meeting point. Cars were swishing by on the wet A20 below me, their tail lights pursued by a red haemorrhagic spray as I sat all alone in a beaten up Transit van in a lay-by on the B something or the other; a little used road chosen for that very reason.

What the bloody hell was I doing at this time of night at my age, spearheading this caper just for a couple of grand commission I was more than half convinced that I should never see? The Jag arrived spot on time, pulled over and rolled silently to a halt as Daniel in a white Burberry raincoat, with the collar turned up, sauntered round to the near side of the van. I pulled my hood up on my anorak and joined him.

"Hi," he said visibly relieved that I was alone. He pulled out a silver foil covered packet at random from the boxes in the back of the van, and began to examine its contents while I balanced the briefcase which he had handed to me on the parapet. I thumbed the catches. My god it was beautiful, all that cash. The case was tightly packed with it and by rights 2.5% of it was mine. I still harboured doubts and shivered, but not just with the cold.

I had just clicked the case shut when the world exploded into a nightmare of screeching tyres, flashing blue lights and slamming doors. I did not need to turn around to know that a whole crew of serious young men in flak jackets were pointing Heckler and Kotch machine pistols at the back of my head. I stood there frozen with my hands on my head and fingers locked, just like in the movies. I turned to face the music, and in doing so the briefcase tumbled silently into the darkness below.

"Don't say a word, Daniel," I said. "Let me do all the talking."

"Yes," he said. "I think that would be best if you did the talking.

I will, however, say just one thing."

"And what's that?"

"Sorry, Jimbo. You need not say anything unless you wish to do so but it may harm your defence if you do not say anything when questioned, which you later rely on when giving evidence." The rest was a blur, until an elderly gentleman in a Crombie overcoat stepped out of a black BMW. On his way to the opera no doubt.

"Well done Chief Inspector Daniels. Nice collar."

"Thank you Super, I've had my eye on this one for some time. Record as long as your arm."

"Well, can't hang about; meeting the Home Secretary for supper and a spot of Stravinsky at Covent Garden, and I'm a bit late already."

Well I was right about the opera if nothing else.

"OK you men, take him in."

"Book him Danno," I said to myself as I was shoehorned into the rear of a squad car. Just before the door slammed shut I heard the Chief Superintendent say to Daniel, "Best I take care of the money now. We don't want that going astray in the divisional canteen now do we? ha ha."

I wish that I could have seen their faces when they looked to find it gone, but it was not to be as we were blasted off towards Maidstone at high decibels. Even under lock and key far, far away Mr Churchill is the consummate professional, he thinks of everything and was not about to let an upstart like Seth Hardcastle pull a deal of this size on his turf. God alone knows how he found out that it was a police sting operation, but he did. A spy in the camp no doubt.

Whatever was in the van apart from a few packets on top it wasn't top notch cannabis resin. It could have been marzipan for all I cared, still there was enough of the real stuff lying about to get me sent down, but released upon appeal. The element of police involvement raised the question of entrapment, and the bewigged wise old bird on the bench declared the conviction unsafe and so off I went.

Below the flyover that damp and windy night sat a large man in an all-weather motorcycle suit astride a dark Honda moped, rain dripping from his ghastly medieval features, patiently waiting until a briefcase full of money dropped into his arms. Having crossed Mr Churchill once before, many years ago, there was no way that he would even contemplate doing so a second time. As it was he would never play the violin again.

IPS⊕ FACT⊕

I don't know what all the fuss is about. I mean to say, if the boys in my old school are anything to go by. In those days if some randy vicar had started laying on of hands uninvited he could have expected a red hot Woodbine in the eye for his trouble. Either that or a rusty razor blade where East meets West if you get my drift, giving a whole new meaning to the term great schism. We were a pretty straight-laced lot back then in South London. A highly developed sense of the proprieties you might say, within reason that is.

There were a couple of dirty little buggers like Kenny Tarrot and Roger Allenby with their tame little catamite, but I don't think that even they had much to do with men in holy orders. But that was long before vicars started riding motorbikes and playing guitars in coffee shops. Even today I suspect that invitations to take a walk on the wild side would only be directed at, and be favourably received by, brats who were more than half way left wing to start with.

So it's a bit cruel that having taken the muddy sacrament they then blow the whistle and cry abuse. One eye on a big cheque from the Red Top press like as not, either that or they see it as a way to get a job with the BBC.

It was under similar circumstances to these that Father

O'Flaherty took up residence on the landing below mine with a heavy six to look forward to. He was not allowed to wear his dog collar in here of course, but even so quite a few old lags looked to him for some sort of spiritual leadership in preference to the ministrations of our regular chaplain.

The others, well, you know what the pecking order is like in here with our perverted parson on the bottom rung. His six years was going to feel like sixty if he should live that long. Well serves him right. I had worries of my own to worry about at that time, having been a party to killing the Governor's cat which we had made up into a fur hat before selling it to Ivan the Red as genuine Scottish bear cub fur.

The Governor recognised his tabby immediately, confiscated the hat and started an enquiry. At the same time Ivan wanted his money back and was backing up his consumer complaint with very real threats of Stalinist-inspired violence. One thing I could have done without just then was a summons to see the all-powerful Mr Churchill for a little chat.

As I have said before, he treated me reasonably well. Well for a homicidal megalomaniac that is. I had seen the former reverend O'Flaherty enter his cell earlier that day and half expected to see him licking Mr Churchill's hand-lasted Oxford brogues and polishing them to a parade ground shine with his shirt. I paused in the doorway, having been allowed thus far by Three Fingers Bone - his minder.

"Come in, Jimbo. Sorry that you are too late for tea."

"Sorry if I am a bit late, Mr Churchill," I replied, although I wasn't the least bit late or sorry having no choice in the matter.

"Was it something important you wanted to see me about?"

"All in good time, Jimbo, all in good time. Do you speak Latin by the way?" he said munching on the last of his tea time Jaffa Cakes.

"Er, no Mr Churchill. Not much call for it in Peckham."

"Pity - great pity. Every well-educated man should speak Latin, don't you agree?"

"Oh yes essential I should say," I replied, wondering where all this was leading. There had to be a scam at the back of it somewhere, but for the life of me I couldn't think what it was.

"Have you met Mr O'Flaherty? I see that you have. Well let me be brief. The reverend here is teaching me Latin – "*pro bono publico.*"

O'Flaherty looked up and gave the sort of smile I recognised from the BBC's presentation of *David Copperfield.* You must know who I mean. Uriah Heep. That's the chap. Ever so humble he was. No doubt in my mind about it, this poor excuse for a man was a sodomite slug.

"All very commendable Mr Churchill, but I can't see how this affects me, I don't speak Latin."

"Didn't suppose that you did, Jimbo, but to cut to the chase - *praemonitus - praemunitus* as we say don't we Vic?"

Another greasy grin which nearly turned my stomach.

"Thing is Jimbo, there are some fellow travellers in this here institution who would gladly separate this man of God from his holy relics, and I will not find that amusing or convenient."

And neither would O'Flaherty I thought, but said nothing.

"So I want you to take him under your wing so to speak."

This was not a mission I could view with any sense of equanimity. I mean to say, I had a social position to maintain in here. And whilst I was quite capable of giving a bit of a slap to many of my colleagues, and there were others that I could keep at arm's length through humour, writing the odd letter for them and so forth. There were also people like the Bugden brothers; great muscle-bound brutes who, if they want to take the piss or take anything at all, will do so and it would be unrealistic to imagine that I could fob them off with witty repartee.

No. I just wasn't going to put up with it. Nursemaid some diabolical defrocked deacon. No way. Not on your life. Not in a million years.

"Err, not really my sort of thing Mr Churchill. Perhaps if you asked Bone or better still Grinder, he genuflects at the same altar, he would love to do it. Even pay for the privilege I expect. Right up his street." These two being a couple of Mr Churchill's regular minders, and Grinder was rather partial to botty bacon himself.

"Ha ha. Jimbo you are really a wag. The gentlemen to whom you refer are at the top of the tree and I for one would not demean them by asking either one to attend to such a trivial matter. One day you will learn, Jimbo, that the art of command is not to give orders which are sure to be refused. It places the status quo at risk. Status quo, that's Latin, right? I am no longer a young man and the day will come when, and one day I will have to ..."

Realising that he had already revealed more of his innermost insecurities than was prudent, he shut up.

"This is your thing, this one is all for you, because I say it is.

Now don't disappoint me. You are NOT going to disappoint me are you?"

"No, no, course not Mr Churchill."

"Close the door on your way out Jimbo."

Walking back to the relative sanity of my cell, I passed Colin Dipwick and his cell-mate Ray the Rape, who began to grin. How they knew of my new commission I had no idea, but news is not slow in passing in stir.

I am a man of peace. Ask anybody. A man of peace. Peace, peace, peace. I might even have said it out loud as I punched Colin Dipwick square on the nose and half turning gave Ray the Rape the benefit of a left cross to the side of the head, then gave Colin another one, not so hard this time as he had his hands over his bloody face, and moved off promptly back to my cell without further unspoken criticism or censure from any quarter.

A couple of hours later, after the vicar had permanently attached himself to my coat tails like a personalised ball and chain, he decided that he must go to the bog. He would wouldn't he?

Passing by a couple of heavy old lags playing Ludo, one of them who thought himself no end of a wit shouts out, "Horny swaz key melly ponce!"

To which I replied, "Oh is that what you are in here for Wilson – poncing? I thought it was flashing on the underground." Actually it was robbery with violence, but it got a laugh from the other prisoners within earshot.

A bit of a weak response I know, but there was no way I was going to get into a bounce-up with a bloke his size, even if he was ten years or more older than me . He got up a bit lively, upsetting the Ludo board.

There were lots of side bets on the outcome and Elvis Postlethwaite, who had staked his small all, cried "Cheat!" and took a poke at the lumbering Wilson, who returned the compliment with some verve and all hell broke loose. The screws were on them in seconds, whilst the Sick-Vic and I made our excuses and left for the bogs as quietly as possible. Was I expected to go through this routine every time he wanted to take a leak?

I had had more than enough of this lark already and it was still the first day, but how to extricate myself from the situation I hadn't a clue.

If you have small children, you will know what the routines of parenthood are like.

You drop the little blighters off at the school gates, pick them up again when class is out to see that they don't get roughed up by their schoolmates on the way home. It could have been a whole lot worse, but the couple of slaps I handed out on day one set the scene. Either that, or the news that he was ultimately under the protection of Mr Churchill, kept him from harm. But having said that I cannot vouchsafe for what they did to his food or what went into his tea, but that was not my concern and frankly I couldn't give a snuff.

One day I asked him how the lessons were going and what sort of pupil Mr Churchill was turning out to be.

"His verbs are rather weak, but he has quite a good memory for trivia. If he finds a Latin tag he repeats it endlessly. "Carthage must be destroyed!" was a particular favourite with him, and when I asked him if he knew where Carthage was, he waived an imperial hand in the air and replied somewhere in the Roman Empire where they speak Latin of course. As I did not wish to have to branch out into instructing him about the geopolitics of the ancient world, I kept quiet on the issue. Neither could I make him quite understand that certain English idioms will not translate directly into Latin and that explaining what they meant is convoluted and tedious.

"The sages of antiquity never had the need to 'Bung the old bill. Have it away. Push the snide, Cut the nose candy or take a punt'. Although I dare say, Jimbo, that the *mobil vulgus* had an equally arcane argot all their own. I can't see him taking his O-Level any time soon, but even so I fail to see what it is all for. I mean it seems unlikely that he wishes to convert to Catholicism, and should he have some idea of an audience with the Holy Father in Rome, what would be the purpose and what on earth would they talk about ?"

"You tell me Vic," I replied. "There is more GBH, murder, incest and various other hanky panky in the good book than you can shake Aaron's Rod at."

"No."

"Oh yes! Murder - Cain. Infanticide - Herod. Conspiracy to theft and kidnapping - Joseph's brothers. Incest – Noah. Even Jesus wasn't above a bit of vandalism."

"Oh no, not our Lord."

"Uh yes, your Lord. Have you forgotten what he did to some poor bugger's fig tree on the outskirts of Bethany?"

"Oh, you know about that! But he only did that to ..."

"Cool it, Vic. You don't have to explain it to me. I'm no magistrate, but that sort of behaviour is worth an ASBO in my book. If Mr C wants to go to Rome it is only to case the joint. He probably has a fleet of mini cars on order this very minute and some poor punter is doing a reconnoitre of the Roman sewers even as we speak. It's all a lot of old tosh. Now shut up. I want to take a nap."

"He's up to something. You mark my words."

So he was, but I couldn't for the life of me work out what sort of scam he was up to and it will come as no surprise to you that I was well and truly sick of the whole business and ready to flee to the land of dreams at every opportunity. Some weeks later, following a night of passion with Carol Vorderman in my Persian Palace, I awoke to what promised to be a most enterprising day. I dropped the Vic at Mr Churchill's cell door and starting out with half a tin of Cherry Blossom, I traded up via a Mars bar, three ballpoint pens and a bar of Cadbury's fruit and nut, to a brand new pair of Argyle socks, so as you may imagine it was not a day wasted. Wasted as things go in here that is, and being Friday I still had fish cakes and chips to look forward to at lunch time.

As I was on the way back to my bijou penthouse suite at the Greywall Hilton, the door to Mr Churchill's cell flew open and out flew my ward, a delightful bruise just starting to show around his left eye. A second later the great man himself comes out with an armful of books which he proceeded to fling with no small force at the rapidly departing ecclesiastical head. First the landing, and then the whole wing fell dead quiet.

What he shouted might have been English, Latin, Serbo-Croat or Zulu for that matter, but it was evident beyond dispute that he was rather cross. I tried to slip past unnoticed as the screws came clumping up the metal stairs to see what was occurring, but a great hand reached out, grabbed me by the sleeve and pulled me.

"Ah Jimbo," he said. I cannot say that he was any less cross but his anger was, to a minute degree of safety, under restraint. It would not take a great many ill-considered words however to put the kettle back on the boil and I had no wish to get scalded.

"Tell me, if you please Jimbo, what you know about Latin America?" he asked from behind clenched teeth.

Oh, here we go, my starter for ten.

"Not a great deal Mr C. Just about what everyone knows. It's all the countries from Mexico southwards. Mostly Catholic countries with large populations, most of whom live in poverty. Chile is mostly mountains and bird droppings called guano which they export lots of, as fertilizer don't you know. Argentina produces a lot of beef. They grow a lot of dope of various kinds in Peru and Colombia. Famous for pretty girls that is Colombia. Ecuador produces all the world's Panama hats. You would think it was Panama but for some historic reason Panama produces very few hats, but it has the canal and is also the world's largest..."

"Shut your bleeding trap! Wittering on about hats and bird shit."

He paused, his anger only just short of erupting with volcanic violence.

"Language. Tell me what language they speak?"

Suddenly the penny dropped, and I knew that if I so much as betrayed the merest hint of a smile I would get a leg broken or, if whichever minder he sent to "do me" didn't like Argyle socks, maybe both legs. I thought about dentists. I thought about Edward the 2nd and red hot fire irons. About the death of Bambi's mother and other imagined painful things too private to tell of.

It worked, for with the straightest of faces I said "Spanish mostly. Except for Brazil that is, where they speak Portuguese." "Then why do they call it Latin America?"

I could have told him about the treaty of Saragossa which divvied up the New World between Portugal and Spain, but when I had said that I would have told him all I knew and wished to avoid the lacuna which would have inevitably followed, so I decided to keep quiet.

Unnecessarily so as it happened for he said, "No, don't answer that because I don't bloody well care. Mr Georges Escobar must have thought it a right bloody joke when I at last got him to the telephone this morning and started to negotiate a concession in bloody Latin. It cost me five hundred cigarettes to get the exclusive use of that line in the library. And when I starts spouting Latin at him he didn't understand a bloody single word. He must have taken me for a right gibbering idiot. That vicar is going to pay for this with his thuribles."

Thuribles. That was a word I would never have thought to have heard from Mr Churchill, but that's what happens if you break bread with men of the cloth on a regular basis; you pick up all sorts of things.

He threw a tea cup. One of his best, Crown Derby, against the wall. An uncharacteristic show of anger. Mostly he shows no emotion at all, even when he orders someone to be beaten to a pulp. I had to think quicker than I had ever thought before. and I can think quicker on my feet than most.

"No, no, not at all Mr C, he probably thinks that you were showing off your education, putting a poor uneducated Columbian in his place. For all his millions. he is still a peasant worth tuppence in a market with shit at four pence a pound. Either that or he thought that you were connected with the

Italian Mafia, speaking with a heavy Corsican accent."

"Mafia eh? You really think so, Jimbo?"

"And it won't do your credibility any harm will it, if you take a high hand and play it real cool for a bit then get back to the cartel when you have had time to fix up a proper interpreter?"

"Jimbo. you are brilliant. A genius. How can I thank you enough? There was a time there when I was feeling a right prat and you kindly put it all into perspective for me. Tell me now. How can I ever repay you?"

"Well if you have had enough of these Latin lessons I would be glad not to have to babysit the vicar anymore."

"No bother Jimbo, he is being shipped out for his own safety to Channings Wood, a low security category C prison near Newton Abbot wherever that is."

"It's in Devon Mr C, you know where that is, close to Dartmoor, it's where the Cornish Pasties go during the mating season."

"Grinder was most cut up about it, Jimbo. He had high hopes in that direction. He never even said good-bye."

"*Abit nemine salutato*, as we scholars say Mr C, and bloody good riddance, as we say in Peckham."

THE SPIRIT ⊕F ENTERPRISE

In these strained economic times it must be most reassuring to the general public to learn that the spirit of enterprise is not dead in the hearts of proud and industrious men.

One only has to look at the number and variety of SMEs, that is small to medium enterprises, which are spawned to flourish within the walls of Her Majesty's further education establishments - to wit - the nick.

That these places have made up the alma-mater of so many of our up and coming young businessmen is self-evident and I have described some of these elsewhere, although ever one for a quiet life I seldom take an active part in any of them.

Mr Churchill, as you know, has an established corner in financial matters, AKA the loan shark business, plus more fingers in more pies on A wing than he has fingers. Toes too I shouldn't wonder. Over on E wing, Rasta Johnson is the retailer of mark for any number of irregular substances not found in a conventional pharmacopeia. Poppers, uppers and downers, you name it he can supply it, a regular multi-coloured chemical magic carpet to take a body far away from these grey damp high walls to where the skies are blue, the grass is green and coconuts fall from the trees in the balmy warm breezes. A

Shangri-La where "the white pigs don't get in ya face when you aint done nuffink."

Two inmates on my landing, Brian Phillips and Malcolm Rubbins, had a nice little racket in recycled rubber goods. Don't ask, just use your imagination. Whatever your taste or inclination there are always people ready to fill the need. At a price of course. The law of supply and demand is one of the few pieces of legislation to hold sway in here. One little piece of business I was reluctantly involved in was Charlie Young's Brewery. A significant and long-awaited addition to the grey economy.

Alcohol, as you are no doubt aware, is a by-product of yeast-type organisms as they digest carbohydrates, preferably sugar; both ingredients being readily, if illicitly, available from the prison kitchens and bakery.

A two-pound bag of sugar, a handful of yeast and a slop bucket carefully placed on the heating pipes, and Bob's your uncle. Strain the resulting gunge through a nylon sock, add a dollop of tomato sauce for colour and hey-presto a gallon of Chateau Piss Pot at a pound a pint. Woodbines taken in lieu.

It was, I suppose, a nice little earner as these things go, and as all good things go, it went. It went because word drifted along the various landings until it was brought to the attention of Mr Clarence Churchill, who took a sip which he rolled around his discerning palate for a moment before spitting it into a paper cup, pronouncing that in his mature and considered opinion, this was a product worthy of an infected civet cat, but that it had a certain "*je ne sais quoi*" and worth a punt. That is to say further investment of capital and enterprise to capitalise on an expanding and captive market.

Well it was none of my biz if Mr Churchill wished to dispossess

Charlie Young of his. None of my business, that is, until I was summoned to a royal audience with his awfulness.

"Earl Grey Jimbo?" he enquired, his voice as dulcet as scrap iron in a cement mixer.

"Er, no thanks Mr Churchill." It always being an error to accept largesse from sadistic monsters with a touchy sense of their own generosity.

"No? Well take a seat then."

I sat.

"You two outside. See we are not disturbed. Jimbo and I have important matters to discuss," this to his two minders / bodyguards, Three Fingers Bone and Bread Knife Baker. They grunted ascent, and left leaving me to wonder what mad scheme he had cooked up now to further endanger my chances of an early release. It came as no real surprise to see that he held my P101 file in his hand lifted from the governor's office. Whatever he wanted he usually got. Except his freedom that is.

"It says here, Jimbo, that you are something of a scientist; a biochemist is that right?"

"No, not in a million years, Mr C. It must be a mistake."

"No mistake, Jimbo," he said, spitting out a pip from his lemon tea.

"It's here in black and white. Sprules Road Secondary Modern School, London SE4 where you obtained a valuable qualification in Chemistry and Biology. So?"

"Oh, yes, but that was just the leaving certificate, not even a

GCE, and anyway it was donkey's years ago. I can't pretend to be a chemist."

His voice changed gear and dropped an octave as if I was being obstructive. There was steel in his tone, rusty but sharp. I knew better than to argue the finer points of the education system.

"I ain't asking you to pretend, but you're the nearest thing we have to a chemist in here you see, and if I ask you nicely to..."
He didn't have to say any more for suddenly I could add intern chemist to my CV.

What he wanted didn't take much by way of a chemical education. When his boys had muscled into Charlie's operation they up scaled from gallon sized slop buckets to full sized dustbins in the boiler room. This would have worked had the bins been clean, but they were filthy, which resulted in a dark yellow scum which sat atop the brew, which was as unpalatable as it looked and undrinkable even by the standards of the rank and file aficionados in here.

Boiling water, bleach and a whole packet of industrial sized Brillo pads soon sorted that one out and earned me a two-ounce tin of Old Holborn as a reward, and quite reasonably I thought that my troubles were over and so they were for a few quiet weeks. As you may know, I enjoy peace and quiet. A few good books and no interruptions from either the screws or the likes of Mr Churchill.

Then I received my second summons just as H G Wells's time traveller had dragged a fair haired little Eloi maid called Weena from the river. Saved her from drowning and was about to demonstrate some of the psycho-sexual deviant behaviour that unmarried scientists were prone to in the 1880's.

Cursing silently under my breath - I dare not do otherwise - I followed Mr Churchill's herald, Bread Knife Baker, along the landing and up three long flights of iron stairs to his pied-à-terre. Wishing that I had a time machine every step of the way, I entered in a state of great trepidation.

"You wanted me Mr Churchill? Nothing amiss with the vintage I trust?"

With a twitch of a thumb he dismissed Mr Baker.

"It's not good, Jimbo. Sales have flattened out and I need your help to..."

What did he want me to do now? Grow real grapes on the prison farm and have them pressed by bare footed inmates?

"Add value. Yes, that is what we must do, add value, as they say on Madison Avenue."

For a while I didn't get his drift. What did he want from me?

The design of a classy label with an endorsement from Lucretia Borgia. I was not in a state of mystification long.

"What we must do is distil it."

I suddenly went cold inside. This is what "WE" must do was it? I must have looked uncomprehending, when in fact I was terrified of what compliance would do to my chance of early release if discovered, and equally terrified of what would happen to my bodily appendages if I refused to cooperate.

"You know all about distilling I am sure. Turn it into vodka, gin, rum or whisky. I am sure that you can do it. You have my complete confidence."

An innocent phrase designed to encourage, but what I heard was the meaning behind the mere words.

"Cock it up and I'll have you drowned in it."

To cut a long story short, Mr Churchill managed by proxy, as was his wont, to assemble the copper coil, tea urn and various other essential bits and pieces. He even sourced a little gizzmo to test the strength of the product.

A week later we were in full production. A dustbin full of liquor would render down into about three gallons of hooch. I was careful to see that it burned with a blue, and not a red, flame indicating that it was ethyl and not methyl alcohol and would not send the customers blind, even if the taste coupled with the strength would shrivel the whang of a walrus. It would, I suppose, serve a purpose. The contents of bottles coloured with a tea bag and sold as whisky were particularly popular, even though they cost more.

By about the fifth or sixth batch I was starting to get worried. The screws were bound to find out eventually what was being cooked up in the boiler room, and if I was caught in charge I would never get out of this rotten place.

So I took a leaf out of Mr Churchill's book and got some other mugs to do all the work. Do you know, the quality actually improved? Sales went up and I had to instigate a three shift system to keep pace with demand. Mr Churchill was well pleased, but surely even he didn't think that the business could go on expanding for ever.

Were you aware that in Brazil they run their cars on alcohol? Fuel is vaporized in the carburettor, mixed with air, compressed and ignited by a spark. The resulting series of violent explosions propels Fernando's Volkswagen down the Via Dutra at a great rate of knots. An indication of just how powerful alcohol can be. If distilled under less than optimum circumstances, a percentage of raw alcohol escapes into the atmosphere. This is known as the angels' share.

One of the best men on the team was a murderer called Double Diamond Derek. He had such a list of victims to his credit, mostly from his wife's family, that it was a safe bet that he was never going to get out. I always had a soft spot for young Derek, after all murdering an unfaithful wife is not the same as topping some poor old age pensioner with a sawn off shot gun when a post office robbery turns sour. Though why he had to go on and do her sisters, her cousins and her aunts as well remains a mystery. He never said, and I never asked.

On the day in question, Double Diamond Derek was labouring away silently in the cavernous boiler room, the air heavy with escaped fumes. He began to feel as if prison wasn't such a bad place after all. Time for a little break to catch his breath and count his many blessings. He had not felt this lightheaded and euphoric in ages. A most pleasant experience and one which could only be enhanced by a few puffs of the joint he had been carefully saving. Not having a lighter handy he opened the door of the boiler.

There was a blinding flash. The pressure vessel took off like a Sputnik. The vat full of alcohol exploded with no small violence, sending shards of metal in all directions. The back of the boiler blew off, as did the boiler house door. A twenty-foot diameter hole appeared in the exercise yard, and fire engines from three counties turned up in a matter of minutes to join in the fun.

Such evidence of the still as there may have been was destroyed in the fireball, or hidden beneath the rubble. The screws conducted an investigation of course, and put the whole thing down to a gas leak. How could they be expected to know that it was a coke fired boiler.

Mr Churchill, having got back considerably more than his initial investment, drew a line under the whole business and laid low for some time, eventually reaching the conclusion that the bootleg booze business was not for him, and turned his considerable talent towards bookmaking; much more his style and one which did not bring my name to the forefront of his mind. Thank God.

One business dies and the plucky green shoots of others spring up to take its place in the sunshine. Proof, if proof were needed, that the spirit of enterprise is not yet dead.

Unlike poor young Derek of course, who is officially listed as missing and presumed to have escaped. Which in a way I suppose that he has.

TWO LEGS BAD
FOUR LEGS GOOD

It was during my first stretch in HMP Greywall, when I was still a bit green in the ways of the world under lock and key, that I thought that it would be an incredibly pleasant way to while away three years if I were to be a helper in the prison library, but green as I was, I had no conception of the pressures that exist in these places to blight such anticipated pleasures.

But I had no way of knowing that then, and got my application in the same morning that it became common knowledge that a vacancy existed.

My first interview was with the prison governor, Mr Eldridge it was back then, who advised me that whilst there were any number of applicants for the post, there were few who had the right qualifications. The right degree of literacy and so forth. It mystifies me even to this day why someone who can barely read and write his own name would wish to work in a library. But there you have it, just one of the incongruities of prison life.

Whilst he made no promises he told me that it looked like being a two horse race. An even contest between myself and Dr Lukabinda.

Bright chap that Lukabinda. Lots of experience of working with books, and with many well placed supporters in here. Come to that I was not without supporters myself, but how much I could depend upon them would remain to be seen.

At the end of the day it all boiled down to the final interview with the librarian, Mr Alexander.

In due course with sparkling spectacles, clean shirt and polished shoes I presented myself for the interview. To be on the safe side I arrived ten minutes early. Security scares and lock downs could delay anybody these days, but I need not have worried as I had plenty of time in hand. If truth be told I had nothing but time as things stood, and had to pace up and down in the exercise yard for a while under the eagle eye of the warden, Mr Soaper, who started work here at about the same time as I arrived. He was almost as green as I was. It would be several years before his natural idealism was transformed by the harsh school of realism into hard bitten cynicism.

Upon arrival I had been befriended by a long term resident called Mr Clarence Churchill who seemed to have everything in hand. From the way other prisoners and some wardens deferred to him, it was evident that he carried a lot of weight around here, although I must confess that his constant companions were not a pretty pair. Horrendous basilisks are the names I would use now, but back then I was, as I have said, a bit green. He, Mr Churchill, stood by the entrance to the office block that housed the library trying to look inconspicuous. A barracuda in a birthing pool might have more success in hiding its true nature.

I walked through the waiting room where a short fat woman called Miss Gully sat typing. I found it difficult to convince myself that in six months I would not find her the sexiest woman on the planet. At the open door to the librarian's office I paused to collect my thoughts and try to remember what I could of the Dewey Decimal system, which - to be honest - was not a lot. A voice from the outer corridor growled, "Good luck Jimbo."

"Come in, come in - don't just stand there. Please sit down. Er, James, isn't it? Yes, well sit you down and make yourself comfortable."

I sat on the far from comfortable utility brand tubular chair and stared at the clutter on his desk. To the right of a small Venetian glass vase of early spring flowers sat an engraved silver cigarette box just out of reach. I hoped that he would offer me one. Not that I smoked myself, but cigarettes are very useful things to have in here.

"Earl Grey or Assam?" he asked. "Help yourself to biscuits," pushing a plate of chocolate digestives in my direction with an effete flourish. I took one, wishing that I could cram them all into my pockets.

So there we sat, the two of us, for quite a few minutes drinking lemon tea and feeling no end of a lemon myself.

He wittered on a bit about the mess the gardeners had made of his roses in the courtyard. Overwatering, magnesium deficiency, fungus, aphids and tools which were being constantly lost or misplaced. "Found a pruning knife in the kitchen the other day, remarkable. What do you think it was doing there do you suppose?"

I raised my eyebrows in disbelief.

He went on to ask if I knew of any enthusiastic gardeners amongst the inmates he might take on. I didn't, but said that I would make enquiries.

The second hand on the big Bakelite wall clock jerked resolutely forward with a mute clunk, and a pigeon landed on the windowsill outside looking for all the world like a chinless parson in search of a congregation before fluttering off. How I envied him his freedom of movement.

The hard seat was getting a little more than uncomfortable. Would this man ever stop rambling on? No doubt he thought that he was being matey, but my god he was talking about his missing socks or something now. Please, please, please just ask me something about books. *The Man in The Iron Mask*, *The Count of Monte Cristo* or *Papillion*, all favourites of mine. Apart from *The Colditz Story* that is.

What was I doing here? After all, there were other jobs I might have applied for. Perhaps I really would be happier doing something else. Pig farming perhaps. They say that once you get used to the smell, pigs make excellent companions. Working outside in the fresh air would have been heaven just about then. Together we reached for the last biscuit. I let him have it. Silly not to. He saw me start to fidget on the hard plywood seat although I had been squirming for some time.

"Do you suffer from haemorrhoids?" he asked.

"Er, um, no," I responded. "Why, do you?"

"No, no, no, but Mrs E has a spot of bother from time to time, but she has this marvellous cream, absolutely excellent don't you know. She'll be here in a little while. Always drives me to the Rotary Lunch on Fridays."

'I must remember to ask after her piles', I thought, knowing that I would do no such thing.

"Lots of sitting down you know in the library business. But if you're sure, well enough said. When can you start? Right away?

Well … excellent, good 'o."

That just had to be about the strangest interview I was ever at. His austere overweight secretary brought matters to a conclusion by entering to advise him that the local MP was on the telephone to have a quick word about his son, Gerald, who had just this morning been sent down for long-shop fraud and would be joining us for a long stay sometime soon.

"Thank you," I said, standing, offering my hand and adding not quite seamlessly, "Sir."

His handshake was a lot less than firm, but I supposed that there must be some fibre in him somewhere to hold and keep the job that he had. Suddenly the ordeal was over and the air in the exercise yard was refreshingly chilly after the stuffy overheated office.

"How did it go?" enquired a slow, dark voice.

"Oh, Mr Churchill, very well I... I got the job. Dr Lukabinda suddenly dropped out at the last moment."

"I know."

"Did he say why he dropped out?"

"Not to me he didn't. Did he say anything to you boys?"

"He said he couldn't possibly hold on a moment longer Boss."

"Well there you have it, he simply lost his grip. Stand aside boys let the ambulance men through."

"I start in the morning."

"Oh good - it is good isn't it boys?"

The boys nodded.

"Now as we are both here, shall we have a little audit?"

"Audit?" I repeated.

"Yes audit, a reckoning, a summing up, a balancing of the books."

"Oh yes," I said. "An audit."

"Let me see now," he said resorting to an aide memoir in the form of a little red pocket book, withdrawing a miniature pencil from its spine, the point of which he proceeded to lick with a tongue like an over-generous slice of bratwurst."

Fixing me with his cold eyes he continued, "May the second. Two ounces of snout to have that bloke what's been pestering your bird, sorry, your young lady, back in London, dissuaded. Sorted. He'll not be back. June. An ounce of snout for keeping the butch butterflies away while you enjoy a nice refreshing shower. July, August, September, Ditto Ditto Ditto. Which brings us to today's little fixer. Three half pound bars of fruit and nut and a bottle, a large family-sized bottle, of Vosene." He made a fresh note in his little book.

"That is the total of the capital sum," he said pronouncing each word slowly and with great deliberation. "Isn't it boys?"

The boys nodded.

"Now the interest," he said even more slowly.

Interest by God. Was I to be in debt for ever to this monster who has seemed so friendly at the start?

"I can see that the question of interest is causing you some small agitation. So we must come to an arrangement. That is fair would you not agree?" The boys agreed.

"Firstly, I want unlimited use of the telephone in the library when you are on duty. It is essential that I keep my finger on the commercial pulse of the world outside.

You will arrange for me to have my own copy of *Fanny Hill*, and no pages stuck together or there'll be trouble. And *Lolita* and 'Emanuelle at Henley', 'Debby does the Lib-Dems'. But oh dear me I must not neglect my education and must simply have the classical one, you know 'Slappo Lesbian Boss'."

"I think you mean *Sappho of Lesbos*."

"Yeah that an' all. And while you are at it see if you can get a back issue of *Playboy*. June 1965. My niece Caroline is in that one. Lovely girl, but not a trainee teacher like it says. She works on the ironmongery counter of Woolworths in Peckham. Funny them getting that wrong." Then with a sigh added, "Ugly bitch now of course. Too many kids by too many fathers have done for that wonderful little bod. Bloody shame that. Still. Where were we? One more thing. If that toe rag Rasta Johnson on E Wing gets anything, anything at all before me — well one of these gentlemen", pointing a huge finger at his boys, "Will stamp your library ticket good and proper, need I say more?"

He needn't. I nodded my understanding like a parcel shelf Dachshund.

"Well Jimbo, ta ta. Must push on. Emmerdale Farm in ten minutes." Then turning, added, "You won't forget about the snout and the chocky now will you? So long Jimbo."

At this one of his boys, the one with some of his fingers

missing, drew the side of his thumb slowly down his cheek with a double click of his tongue and a wry smile at the thought of the pleasure to be had should I welch on the debt.

Although there was some small security to be had knowing that I was nominally under the protection of my benefactor, Mr Churchill, whilst in the library, Rasta Johnson was not the sort to concede with good grace that Mr Churchill had a de facto monopoly of the use of the library telephone, which strictly speaking was off limits to all inmates.

Neither was he particularly happy that all of the books with salacious content, real or imagined, ended up lining the bookshelves in Mr Churchill's cell.

As, by long standing arrangement, an out and out war between A and E wing was not on the cards there was only one way Rasta Johnson could make a legitimate protest, which was, as you might imagine, to take out his frustration, by proxy of course, on the librarian of the moment. Three fingers Bone kept them off me once, but I had had enough. Next time they really might cut off, or slice into, something vital when Bone or Bread Knife Baker was not around to come to my deliverance.

By feigning a chronic asthma attack, I was moved first to the hospital wing and then outside to work with the pigs on the prison farm. I forget who took the job in my place, but I wished him luck because he was going to need it.

One day, when all possibilities of repercussions have faded into history, remind me to tell you the story of how I paid off my debt to Mr Churchill by secretly selling a piglet to detective Sergeant Murry for his daughter's wedding. Sad to say I was not invited to the reception, or even received a small slice of wedding cake through the post.

THE GLACIER

He was about the only person in the criminal underworld that Mr Churchill and his goons stood wary of. You did not need to know that he was called the Glacier to have a chill run down your spine upon first acquaintance.

Someone said, not to his face mark you, that he had a smile like an open grave. An observation which, when coupled with those staring stone-like eyes, one could easily credit with veracity that death was his business.

It is fairly common knowledge these days that if you want someone done away with as a matter of expediency the prices start at about one hundred pounds.

Given the present glut of Class A Drugs, a hundred pounds will buy a fair amount of heroin or crack cocaine. A little fixer up front to sharpen the reflexes and focus the mind and the balance upon completion. Believe me, there are any number of junkies out there willing to stick a meat skewer in Granny's neck for a fix or three, if that is all that stands between you and a nice little semi in Battersea or Berkhamsted, but it is dicey, my word ain't it just.

If your budget will extend to £500 you can get a neat workmanlike job from a real assassin. Black as like as not and totally anonymous. You don't even have to pay until the job's done. Well, I mean to say, who in their right mind is going to welch on a debt to a contract killer?

Mind you it takes an awful lot of bottle to even get the word out on the streets of South London and hope that some Lewisham Yeo Boy is going to turn up with a loaded and lightly oiled 9mm Bulgarian Makarov under his armpit. It's not like you can put an ad in the 'Sits Vac' columns of the *Evening Standard*.

"Equal opportunities employer seeks experienced killer. Refs essential, NVQ preferred and oh yes must be computer literate." They seem to want that for everything these days.

They must think that we don't know it is just subtle ageism to stop us old 'uns from applying. Hell's teeth, it's just typing innit. A girl's job. Something to keep the little dears in mascara and rap records until some spotty oik puts them in the club and they can retire forever to a Council flat and a regular stipend from a soft old government. Hey-ho. Such is life in Dumb-Down Britain of the 21st century, but I digress, where was I? Oh yes, hit men.

In this, as in all things commercial, firstly you get only what you pay for and secondly you really do need a recommendation from a satisfied customer. Notice I said customer and not client. To them, the hit men, the client is the poor soul soon to be stretched out on a marble slab prior to having his insides mulled over buy a pathologist and being consigned to the earth, or the flames, to the tune of Abide with Me. Amen to that eh?

It was whilst on remand in Wandsworth that I first learned of The Glacier from Barry the Bigamist, who told me how to get in touch with him should I ever feel the need. This useful piece of information was given in return for my instructing him how to extract alcohol from metal polish by filtering it through several layers of a cotton sock full of crushed charcoal pinched from the art class. Not to my taste but some of the old lags fight over it. Better than nothing if you dilute it 50-50 with Ribena. Cassis for the incarcerated.

'The Glacier'. Ice cold, slippery and heading in a downward direction is how I read it, but he is good at what he does. Leaves nothing to chance. Was not known to the police and will even give you a choice of how you wish things to look afterwards, all at different rates of course. Accident, suicide, natural causes, mugging gone wrong, crime of passion, gangland execution. Whatever suits your purpose best. It's no wonder he is so expensive. He even has a bent Scotland Yard forensic detective on the payroll to advise him what to leave and what not to leave behind on site. I only have this second hand of course, but on one occasion he left behind a broken string of rosary beads and a bloodstained page from the book of psalms. Very costly as you will realise, but so much more secure than mixing it with orcs and junkies. It all depends I suppose on what you stand to gain, offset against what you stand to lose if caught, like twenty years for conspiracy to murder.

Wife or mother-in-law; easy-peasy and worth every penny. Someone better placed in the order of things, like a Member of Parliament or someone likely to be armed or likely to put up a fight, proportionately more. Which is only fair, surely you can see that? The cost has to be balanced against the risk involved. Sitting on Aunt Gloria's chest as you pinch her nose and pour a bottle of gin down her throat in the middle of the night before throwing her down the stairs or popping her into the chest freezer for an hour or so before leaving her, bottle in hand, out on the lawn in her nightgown to freeze to death is a lot less risky than trying to snuff out a game player like Rasta Johnson surrounded by his crew of gun-toting psychopaths, eager to see what their new Glock 9s can do.

There is a phone number which I can sell to you later for a small fee if you are seriously interested, but you don't need me to tell you not to waste his time. If you answer a couple of questions satisfactorily you will be given a code name and an access code to a Ukrainian-based website. Fill out the online questionnaire and about a week later a young lady from Thomas Cook will call you to advise you that your ticket to ... wherever, is ready for collection and off you go.

The Glacier likes to ensure that his customers have a cast iron alibi for when the deed is done. Self-preservation really. Should you be a suspect, you might just make a silly little slip under interrogation and blow the whole deal.

Better by far if you are several thousand miles away on a cruise ship or in a hotel surrounded by the most respectable people. It helps you to be noticed and remembered if you are a colourful character or a big tipper, but this is not essential; just keep your receipts and ticket stubs.

One of his customers, I understand, even managed to get himself arrested for being drunk and disorderly in Malta the evening his nearest and dearest went under a tube train at Leicester Square underground station. Fantastic alibi, but a bit drastic don't you think?

Now the Glacier was just as assiduous with his own alibi. His system was foolproof and works like this. Now for God's sake keep this to yourself. You never heard it from me. Right? OK.

A totally innocent bit-part actor with a striking resemblance to the Glacier, and sworn to secrecy, would from time to time receive a tax free thousand pounds through the post with detailed instructions to be at a certain place at a certain time, wearing a certain suit and raincoat. There he would book into a specified hotel where a room had been reserved for him. On day one he gets himself noticed by spilling red wine on his Burberry, which he takes to the dry cleaners in the town and pockets the ticket. During the next day, he purchases a local newspaper and other odds and ends, and perhaps visits the cinema always remembering to keep the receipts.

Sometime that day or the day after when the client is as stiff as a plank, the actor will receive a text message saying "ET Go Home". Wasting no time, he leaves the hotel, leaving a small cheap suitcase behind and catches the next train to wherever. When the Glacier sees him board the train from a safe distance, he walks back to the hotel, pockets the collection of receipts, bills and newspapers and collects his dry cleaning.

That night he will have a slap-up meal, joke with the waitress about drinking his wine and not washing his raincoat with it, before going to bed and sleeping like a log. Next day he will check out, pay with a credit card and go home.

The population is decreased by one. The Glacier is at least ten thousand pounds up on the week and an unknown actor has been paid incredibly well for taking a short holiday in a neat provincial hotel. A character part in some matrimonial scam or so he believes. Were he to even suspect that he was an accessory to numerous murders he would have a fit. It is very strange to have to admit this, but knowing that there are people like the Glacier about gives me a curious warm feeling. It comes from knowing that if anyone really did take serious liberties with me or mine all I should have to do was shell out five grand or so and take a nice long holiday, and when I came back my troubles would have vanished like the mist in the morning sunshine.

PØCKET VENUS

As by now you will know, I am a man of few emotions and simple habits. I have the history of my childhood to thank for the first, and a life spent on the run or behind bars for the second. That is not to say that my tastes and feelings lack sensitivity or refinement. I like to know, for example, that the whisky decanter is always never less than half full. That there is steak in the fridge and money in the bank. I like my bed sheets lightly starched, and - my financial circumstances permitting - changed daily. An egg or two for breakfast, wholemeal toast, real butter and really fresh strong coffee. All of which is not too much to ask or expect after half a century on this planet, is it? No. But the winds of fortune are fickle and tempest, typhoon and cyclone have conspired to land me in the mire from time to time. The fifteen years out of the last thirty that I have spent behind grey walls under the care and protection of Her Majesty being the most tedious, cruel and debilitating of all. Still, had it not been for well-earned remissions, acquittals and successful appeals it might easily have been twice that.

Phew - after twenty years you come out an institutionalised cabbage, however you stage the instalments. It means months and months watching your back until it becomes second nature, and not just in the showers. Months of converting small advantages into bars of chocolate and fractions of an ounce of Old Holborn. There is always some old lag who will polish your boots for a needle thin cigarette. Others will kiss your arse for only a little more if that's your pleasure. Which is not mine by the way. All that exciting enterprising social free marketing aside, the smell of feet and flatulence are, whatever the do-gooders say, powerful disincentives to re-offend.

I had, thanks to various friends on the outside, a firm offer of a job. A real one, not some adventure with a stocking mask, latex gloves and homemade gelignite. No! This was a proper job. I was to be a salesman - what else? A job with all the usual perks including a company car. All I had to do was sell an ever increasing quota of janitorial supplies. Which translates as brooms, bleach and bog rolls. Could have been a whole lot worse I suppose.

The gates of HMP Greywall crashed behind me for what I hoped would be for the very last time, and I breathed the good clean air of the free. And it tasted great. This had to be my last chance. Another stretch like the last would just about finish me off. Apart from the odd G & T at the Remington Club off Greek Street, in Soho, just for old time's sake, I kept away from bad company as my probation officer said I should. I even, and you won't believe this, I even started going steady with a quaint old-fashioned little muffin I met at night school.

There was even talk of marriage. Well, you have to jolly them along from time to time. You chaps will understand. Give them something to plan for and look forward to, god bless 'em. Don't worry, I would have moved on long before she would ever hear Widow's Toccata. Any port in a storm as the sailors say. Even so it was a simple twice a week, kiss and cuddle relationship. Quite perfect in its way. As I said, I like a little routine in my private life.

There was a "Daddy" of course, an Egyptologist, a man with some serious gelt. No doubt acquired from doing a bit of grave robbing on his own account when he was not on TV cursing the poor labourers who were doing exactly the same thing to eke out a miserable living beneath the hot desert sun. Daddy had set her up with a pleasant little flat in a side street off the Pulham Road. A bit too Habitat for my taste but - OK. OK. If I must I'll come clean. I was tempted, and more than a little at the thought of the provisions of the Matrimonial Homes Act 1987. If I could go the distance and engineer a divorce down the line, I could walk away with about one hundred grand tax free and legal too.

One evening, after a very passable home cooked meal of baby lobster tails, creamed potatoes and fresh runner beans in a rich Normandy butter sauce lifted with just a little paprika, I absentmindedly began to examine some of the bits of antiquarian tat with which her flat was decorated, whilst waiting for the pears in cream and Calvados to appear. Bits of smashed Egyptian pottery for the most part. Not a whole piss pot in the lot. Boring, boring, boring. One piece did catch my eye, however, which I picked up to examine a little more closely; a little calcite statuette of a naked girl with wide hips, and was wondering what this miniature goddess must have been like as a lay when a naked Sandra, all thoughts of pears and Calvados forgotten, pounced upon my back wrapping her thin arms and legs around me and biting my neck.

Coo... if only the reality were one half as erotic as the images forming in your mind right now. But no. A more appropriate image for you to mull over would be that of a Sainsbury's oven ready chicken wrestling with a bulldog puppy in a three-piece suit, no holds barred. Loser does the washing up afterwards.

"For goodness sake girl, let my dinner settle down first," is what I wanted to say, but I never got the chance, for the little clay nymph slipped out of my fingers, span end over end, hit the marble mantle shelf where it split in two, landing among the fire irons where it shattered into a thousand fragments.

"Oh," she said, more surprised than hurt. "That was over three thousand years old - and now you've smashed it."

"Good job it wasn't a new one," I replied turning. She may not have been much of a catch but standing there in the all-together with a silly look on her face and her hands upon her hips I began to feel the old stirring in Adam's Rusty Rifle. I am only human and all those years of enforced abstinence were still fresh in my mind. In that moment a five-foot history teacher with a gamine haircut and come hither eyes filled out the order book quite nicely. So away we went. I nearly spoilt it afterwards by asking if I could have my dessert now.

"I would have thought that was enough of a dessert for any man," she said petulantly, but padded off barefoot to the kitchen returning with dishes and spoons.

"Actually," she said, still naked and without a trace of modesty, "it was a copy. The original, if it could be found would be worth, ooh lots and lots. Daddy says that the original was looted by the Africa Corps back in the 1940s."

And that, pretty much was that, except that she had her wicked way with me once again and if I close my eyes I can still taste the Calvados on that funny little mouth. Was I getting soft on this one?

No. No! Certainly not. Well perhaps yes, just a little bit. Idiot. No. Of course not. Oh hell, I don't know. What a silly thing to ask a chap just after he'd ....

I dropped off to sleep on the hearth rug, had an evil dream and awoke with indigestion.

Although I say so myself I am a pretty good rep and in six months I had a good and expanding book of customers. Top salesman two months in a row. I even had a small toehold in the door of the offices of Persian Gulf Oil Products, but it got off to a very slow start.

You see, if you offer a backhander to the wrong man at the wrong time it's curtains. George, the elderly buying clerk, was a greedy little crook who knew, as he liked to say in a thick Yorkshire accent, "which side his bread were buttered". I could write a book about men on the take. This one was greedy, but cautious, and I wondered just how many free lunches I should have to stand him before I got a decent order.

The next time I called, he was off with a bad back and I had to see his boss, an amiable old Yank who invited me into his office for coffee, where we chewed the fat for half an hour or so, and I left with a small order which was good of course, but the thing which set my pulse racing was a little naked clay Lolita in a glass display cabinet behind his desk.

He saw me looking.

"That," he said. "That little lady could tell you a story. Spoils of war, yes sir, Har Har. I took it off a Limey major in a poker game. It was just one of a whole bunch of stuff he had lifted from a Kraut general. My guys thought I was crazy letting this old boy put this thing up against a pot of twelve hundred bucks, but I had a feeling that I was going to buy the farm pretty damn soon so I didn't care much one way or the other. You young guys should see what an 88 cannon shell can do to a Sherman tank to get some idea of what we went through out there in the desert.

Tommy Cookers, the Germans called them, and damn right they were too. One hit and whoomph - finito. Yes, sir. Your man was cock a hoop with his two pair, Queens and Jacks, but I had two pair as well Queens and Kings and scooped the pot. How's about that for a war story. Don't that beat all."

Over the next couple of months, I did my homework at the British Museum Library and even took a couple of covert snaps of said doll whilst Eugene was out of the room. The hardest part was trying to keep my eyes off the bloody thing when in the company of Eugene at his office. At the same time, I gently pumped Sandra, the love of my life, for information without showing my hand, not that she knew over much.

It's quite a closed world, you know, the world of the Egyptologist, dealer, collector and somehow it soon became common knowledge that I was looking for a fair copy of this diminutive nudist, who by the way turned out to be Tiaa, wife, and - some say - sister, of Amenhotep II, no less.

Eventually I had my copy, and of course somehow Sandra got to hear of it, so I had no choice but to pretend that I had gone to all that trouble to please her, consequently it had to reside for a few weeks on her mantle shelf and of course she had to show her gratitude in the only way she knew how. This time, thank God, before supper. In a way I was going to miss her after I had made my move up to greater things, for she was becoming a habit, but she simply did not fit into the future life I had planned for myself in the sunshine.

At my next visit to Persian Gulf Oil Products it was but the work of a moment to swap the statuettes over and before tea time I had an order for ten dozen cases of two ply, super-soft (white) on the books and the aforementioned little houri safely wrapped in newspaper in my brief case. I had had my eye on one particular dealer for some time. Not your usual antiquarian, but someone I might more correctly describe as a fence and a latter day Fagin. He certainly looked Victorian. Smelt it too. An old brass bell tinkled as I entered the dark and musty near empty emporium where a single unshaded 40-watt bulb at the rear of the shop cast its dusty orange light upon rows of silent clocks, and Zulu spears, while a case of stuffed owls looked on blankly, but sagaciously saying nothing.

I turned the sign on the door to closed and slipped the huge iron bolt. If he was worried, he didn't show it. Probably kept a pistol in his belt, cunning old blighter. I placed my brief case on the counter and thumbed open the locks but before revealing the reason for my visit, with practised ease I pulled a theatrical stunt taught to me by little Albert, one of Mr Churchill's former goons, now no longer with us. I first placed an envelope full of ten pound notes down on the glass counter top, followed by an open cut-throat razor. He looked up puzzled.

"And what's all this?" he said, his hand slipping under the counter to the bell push which I guessed might be there.

"One is a demonstration of good faith and the price of silence. The other represents the cost of indiscretion and loose lips."

"Tell me mister, what do I have to do to earn the one and avoid the other?"

"Nothing." I replied.

"Nothing," he said, incredulous.

"I will know if you have earned your fee without you saying a word."

This was something new in his long experience, a life which had seen kings, dictators and presidents come and go.

I carefully unwrapped my small parcel. Suddenly his old face lit up and his eyes lost about fifty years of worry, and sparkled. He ran his fingers lightly over my pocket Venus and drew breath.

"Oi!" he intoned and answered my unspoken question. As he did so he picked up the envelope with the cash. Smart fellow.

He mumbled something in Hebrew or it might have been Yiddish then, "Where did you get this? This is the real..."

I cut him short by folding the cut throat razor and pressing it to my lips before dropping it back into my case.

He was far too excited not to talk as I had bidden. To me at least.

"I could get you a million dollars for this in Tel-Aviv. Perhaps one and a half or even two in New York."

"Now that is something I shall have to think about Professor. In the meantime, silence is the order of the day. Remember - shtum! As Sandra would have noticed if the copy had suddenly disappeared I thought that the best place to keep the original would be on her mantelpiece. Risky perhaps, but a lot safer there than at my Elephant and Castle flat. A neighbourhood where they steal each other's door mats, urinate over their balconies and leave used hypodermics in the lifts.

Every time I stopped to contemplate the future my heart fluttered like a child's with excitement. By the end of the month I had worked my notice, handed the keys back to my landlord and moved in with Sandra to keep a watchful eye on my treasure, and thought of the best way to dump the randy little dwarf.

Already I could taste the clean plastic smell that large aircraft usually have as it wafted me off to a new life somewhere warm where I would never ever again have to contemplate another winter in Brixton, Parkhurst, Wormwood Scrubs or any place even remotely like them. If I closed my eyes I could feel gentle, warm, salt laden breezes upon my cheeks, hear the soft plash of waves on white coral sand and taste the piña colada. For days on end I was tingling like a highly tuned violin string.

Ah Ah... Ah Ah! Touch me and I shall sing. The little gift and the fact that I had moved in had an incendiary effect upon Sandra. Not that I minded that over much for I was feeling as perky as a prize bull myself. So that on what was to be our last Friday together, not that she knew that, I lay in wait, suitably ossified and did the pouncing for a change. The first bits of clothing came off at the front door and the last bits in the hall and we ended up on the rug by the fireplace as usual. Knowing that this was to be our last tryst I put my heart and soul into my performance. Leave them singing has always been my motto.

Now Sandra, being the crypto-nymphomaniac that she was, was not like other women, happy for a post coital cuddle and a quiet cigarette afterwards. But instead, just like an earthquake, she would experience a series of aftershocks for anything up to half an hour. On the whole it was fun to stand back and watch her writhing, solo antics.

So self-absorbed was she that she didn't seem to miss me when I got up to get a beer from the fridge. I could hear her ecstatic mumblings and chattering teeth from there.

"Oh yes, yes, yes," she moaned as she dug her fingers into a little silk cushion. For a few seconds all was quiet and then she started up again. "Oh yes my darling, Oh my, oh oh! That must be it, I remember thinking to myself, taking a long pull at the beer. She will drop off to sleep directly and Venus and I will quietly tip-toe down the stairs and be on our way to Heathrow with only three hours to check in.

As I thought these words, a further orgasmic aftershock shook her little frame. Why had I taken so much trouble to make her happy this one last time I shall never know, knowing what she was like. Male pride I suppose. I slid my in-flight bag closer to the front door.

"Wheee," she said rolling into a ball before flinging her arms wide and throwing the silk cushion up into the air in one final spasm. Time slowed down like a Tom and Jerry cartoon. It rose up. Touched the light fitting. Shook off a little dust. Deflected. Still spinning. Oh how I counted those revolutions. One, two, three. Its modified parabola, whose destiny was tacit, held my gaze like a cobra. My heart stopped, my breathing stopped.

No. No. No. Please dear god. No. Sweet Jesus I have been good, I have been good, honestly I have. It wasn't stealing. He didn't own it, not really. It belongs in a museum and I would have put it there, not directly of course but. Clearly the Deity was no antiquarian, why should he be, he was the ancient of days for Christ's sake. A little pagan statuette could be as nothing to him in his grand plan and his celestial ear was deaf to my entreaties. As if predestined, my pocket Venus followed her imitation sister into atomised destruction and eternity.

If I had had my cut throat razor to hand I could have sliced Sandra into equally small pieces. I had not cried since secondary school when Crusher Carson took my ... and ... put ... Oh! Never mind, it was all a long time ago.

Tears ran down my face as the sun, sand, seabirds, piña colada, and the broad blue pacific itself gurgled down an infernal dark plughole. A vision made even more horribly bitter by the thought that I had used up all my savings to purchase a first class ticket I could not now use. I had worked my notice; I dropped off the key to my company car and vacated my flat. I had already donated my suits and all my everyday wage-slave clothing to Oxfam.

I was broke, unemployed, carless, homeless and in all probability in breach of the conditions of my probation as well. The tears, once they had started, simply refused to stop. "Oh my darling, my wonderful darling," she said cupping my face in her tiny hands and smothering my damp cheeks in a fusillade of kisses.

"Don't get so upset. It was the loving thought of your gift that mattered. We can always get another copy silly boy. We can take our honeymoon in Egypt, Daddy will pay. We can be there in a week if we get married by special licence. We're bound to find a copy traipsing around all those quaint old bazaars and mysterious little shops full of curiosities."

I sobbed.

"Who knows, my darling, we might even find the original."
I sobbed again.

"There, there, my love, I'll phone Daddy right away to make the arrangements. Mummy will be so pleased. You just sit still for a moment and collect your thoughts."

And sit there I did with my head in my hands and I cried, and I cried, and I cried.

And then I cried some more.

UP ⊕N THE R⊕⊕F

Just about the only thing which may be guaranteed about a prison riot is the media coverage that it attracts. No one really wins because no one has really thought the matter through properly. Not so good at end games, the people in here. Most, but not all, inmates are thick. Which is why they get caught. Why they say anything at all to the arresting officer and why they plead guilty in court just like Lucky Leonard Lloyd.

Mr Churchill, the big cheese, set up a really sweet little job on the outside to relieve a major cosmetics company of many, if not most, of its trade secrets which were kept in a large and impressive looking safe which Sherlock Holmes' adversary Professor Moriarty might have recognised, their vintage being similar. It was not a sophisticated piece of kit to begin with and over one hundred years of wear and tear had surely eroded its self confidence in its ability to secure and protect its cache of priceless trade secrets. Just about any kid from Camberwell could have opened it in five minutes with a bent coat-hanger.

Having got into their offices, done the deed and got out in record time Lucky Leonard pulls off his mask, as cool as you please to light a cigarette before getting into his Ford Cortina as if CCTV had never been invented. It was a relatively new thing back then, but even so it was a pretty daft thing to do.

There must have been squeals of delight coming from the CID room of Carter Street nick when they showed the recording and DI Childers saw that idiotic grin on Lenny's face, which turned to utter bewilderment a few short hours later. He was safely under lock and key before the butter had melted on his tea time crumpet. It was too late, however, to recover the secret formulae for they were on their way to an address in East Cheam prior to being telexed over to Hong Kong. Some three weeks later, although it might have been less. "Rose Bud Blush" was transmuted into "Eastern Sunrise" at half the retail price.

Both unwilling and unable to grass on the brains behind this audacious crime, to wit one Mr Clarence Churchill, and constantly living in fear that said mastermind should ever find out that he has sold photocopies to several turbaned gentlemen at the same time, he could do nothing but keep his mouth firmly shut and take the full five years, like it or lump it.

As I say, there are some thick ones in here. If you add to the prospect of a long stretch all the delightful aromas one might expect where several hundred men are crowded together in cramped and overfull cells, home-cooked dope, sexual frustration and boredom you have all the makings of a riot. Moreover, if the internal restraints are absent all hell can break loose. As it turned out, Rasta Johnson had been given compassionate parole to bury his granny, or so he said. God knows he had never shown anybody compassion in his entire life. A nasty bit of work even by the standards prevailing in here, exemplified by the likes of Pliers Pommeroy and the Cheshire Skinner - Nick Dunn.

By the merest mischance, Mr Churchill - having been requested, with some insistence - to attend Number One Court at the Old Bailey, was on route there under guard with police cars back and front of the prison van when his old trouble flared up with a vengeance and he had to be rushed into Guys Hospital. He said afterwards that he was doing a trial run for an escape later in the year just as soon as the weather warmed up a bit and that the subsequent operation was for an infected toenail. All nonsense of course; he had suffered from the most painful haemorrhoids for years, evil old sod. No doubt caused by his over-rich diet and the effect of stress on his sunny disposition.

The reason that these leaders of the various factions, shadow government if you will, like to keep a lid on unrest in here is that they do not wish to draw attention and adverse publicity to their numerous side-lines. The chief ones being drugs, booze, tobacco and pornography.

So, that was the state of play. Rasta Johnson was away bouncing his wife or somebody else's under the pretext of a family internment. Mr Churchill was skewered on the blunt end of a telescope wielded in the hands of a white coated sadist from Kashmir, which is enough to make your eyes water just thinking about it. Serves him right. Couldn't happen to a nicer fellow.

According to the Six O'Clock News the dispute started over the ownership of a bar of dark chocolate. Later news said a Mars bar or a Kit Kat. I know I said that some of them in here are a bit thick, but they are seldom that daft. Risk all your hard earned remission for good behaviour for a few pennies worth of sweet stuff? Not a chance. But with the gruesome twosome, Johnson and Churchill, out of the picture for a spell, private enterprise took over with respect to the supply of crack cocaine and various other commodities. A bit of an unexpected bonus as it was not an enterprise that would have lasted thirty seconds when they returned. But Kenny Harris refused to pay warden Wilkes his cut for looking the other way. So he, warden Wilkes, confiscated the whole stash. Kenny Harris, having borrowed the cash to finance this transaction from Darren Archer, himself setting up in competition to Mr Churchill, went ballistic and before you can say knife, the TV had gone over the balcony and the kitchen set ablaze.

Alarm bells were ringing everywhere, which was the signal for everyone to start hooting and looting; paying back old grudges and getting in a few new ones. Once the big siren on the roof started up it became serious. When they tried to put the prisoners back in their cells they were resisted, strongly. Mr Hurst followed the TV over the balcony. It could not have been easy or pleasant trying to stand up on the wire mesh stretched between floors and blow a whistle with a mouthful of blood, and two or three broken teeth.

As with conflicts elsewhere in the world, the combatants quickly polarised into their respective camps. People who, by and large, generally got along with the minimum of fuss suddenly threw down their Scrabble tiles and pushed back their chairs like gunfighters in the old west and went at it tooth and claw, and with whatever improvised weapon came to hand.

As you may imagine, with only eleven months left to serve, I made myself scarce PDQ. Sneaking back to the sanctuary of my cell to work on my irregular Spanish verbs I was just in time to discover a lag unknown to me about to have it away with my small stock of twin ply, double soft toilet paper, boot polish and a handful of Bic Biros. Little scrote. I gave him a right-hander to the ear, which he would not forget in a hurry, and the toe of my boot to help him on his way, and shut the door.

With a large bottle of mineral water, some pork scratchings and my trading stock of chocolate raisins and chewing gum, I was all set for a long siege. I tried to return to my irregular verbs but couldn't settle to the task, so I tuned in my little transistor radio and learned that the snow which had started to fall across northern counties would continue, and would probably get worse. At least it was warm in here and heartless rotter that I am I could find no sympathy for the couple of dozen die-hards, sitting, or rather perching, up on the roof pelting the police and the screws with broken tiles.

Well good luck to them I remember saying to an empty cell. No sooner had I closed my eyes and Carol Vorderman was walking towards me along a sun drenched tropical island beach wearing not a great deal, when Mork and Mindy came into my cell without knocking. I suppose that if the Gestapo and the Stasi didn't hold strong views on social calling convention it was a bit much to expect Mr Churchill's minders, Bread Knife Baker and Three Fingers Bone to behave in a more civilised fashion. They were joined a second or two later by Sap. I don't know if that was his real name I only knew him as Mr Churchill's accountant. Whether his name was a reflection on his gullibility or a reference to Standard Accounting Practices I neither knew or cared. I had met him a few times before and found him to be a quiet and inoffensive little man. Most big company embezzlers are of course.

"Jimbo," he said. "What a turn up. Mr Churchill is most concerned. I spoke to him just a few moments ago on the library telephone and he mentioned your name."

Being mentioned by Mr Churchill in any context whatsoever is never good news.

"He has asked me to ask you if you would be kind enough to bring this riot to an end as quickly as possible."

"What!" I nearly bit my tongue off. "Me? You're joking. How for Christ's sake? Ask them to stop being silly boys and trot back to their nice warm cells? He must be potty, or you must think I am."

"He says that your skills as a negotiator are second to none We - um – er," pointing at Mork and Mindy, "have a route open to talk to the authorities. You get what deal you can and then we..." and here he included me in their jolly quartet, "sell it to the boys on the roof."

"That's all very well as far as the herenvolk are concerned, but what if "de bredrin up dare" were deaf to my entreaties and accidentally on purpose let me slide down the slippery roof as a reward for my bloody cheek?"

"Not to worry on that score. Mr Churchill and Mr Johnson have already spoken and heads of terms have been agreed upon, concerning retribution amongst other things. They each have as much to lose as each other should this disturbance be prolonged. A wonderful demonstration if I might say so, Jimbo, of how the races can cooperate in a crisis when their interests are mutual don't you think?"

In my experience they always do cooperate and line their pockets in the process. That is until some interfering son of a bitch starts stirring things up and kicks over the piss pot, and then we all get splashed and walk away stinking. I could not believe how I got involved in this thing, I remember thinking as I crossed the yard to the Governor's office in the administration building with the snow falling and the TV camera floodlights lighting up the walls, and a rough prison blanket around my shoulders feeling like Chief Runamuck last of the Comanches.

Having been frisked for hidden weapons, I was shown first into the governor's office and when he wasn't there out into the cold again over to the incident caravan, a huge office block on wheels which must have cost a fortune. It was quite warm in the little conference area. The governor was there of course in his best heavy weight tweeds and accompanied by numerous other bodies in suits and uniforms, including a politico from the Home Office who seemed to be in charge of the official response.

"Aha, James isn't it - yes. Can you tell me what is it that your comrades want?"

Comrades. That was something original and something I had to put right straight away.

"Comrades? No sir, not comrades. I have taken no part in this disturbance. I have simply volunteered to see if I can be of any assistance to help you to sort things out. Things seem to have gotten out of hand."

"Surely they must have given you a list of their demands?"

"No sir, I doubt that they have had time to reflect as yet on the seriousness of their situation, let alone make any demands."

"What, no demands at all?"

"Yes sir, er, no sir."

Listen to me Yes Sir - No Sir. Three bags full Sir. I will be kissing his arse in a minute. Will that be the right cheek or the left cheek – Sir?

"But if I might suggest some conciliatory gesture on-your part they might..."

"No, no gestures. No concessions. They come down now, immediately or the fire hoses start to spray the roof. No concessions, but we do have warm dry clothing and a hot meal ready for them."

"Do you think that I might have a few moments to think about all this, Sir, and perhaps a cup of tea or coffee and a biscuit?"

"Yes, James, you can have that. Officer Whitworth."

You could see that officer Whitworth didn't like the idea of being sent out for tea and cakes for the likes of me. The tea arrived with a Kit Kat, just a small one, and they left me alone with my thoughts. If I go up there under a flag of truce and say Mr Churchill says cease and desist, the riot will be over in a second. I will be back in my cell with a meaningless thank you to keep me warm, and be pushing a broom tomorrow morning with all the other mugs cleaning up the mess first thing after breakfast. A chore I would just as soon avoid. But if the authorities expected a list of demands I was going to have to think one up. They would have to be reasonable of course. Small inexpensive things.

An extra hour's TV in the evening, some new jigsaw puzzles, less cabbage in the diet and a bit more real meat in the burgers. These and half a dozen other things were whizzing around in my head as I was led up to the top floor. I must admit that I was welcomed with a warmth that surprised me. Most of the lags up there wanted to end this malarkey as much as the authorities did. It was freezing up there, but they had to save face. I went into a huddle over a cigarette with Sparks Watt and Big Victor Gallaway; Cougar Gallaway as he is generally known. They knew that whatever I could get for them they had some stick coming, and there was not a lot I could do about that. I didn't ask them to play silly buggers up here in the cold so they can't blame me for their predicament. I suggested, ever so gently, that Mr C and Mr J would be most grateful if they stopped and went down. I didn't say that they would have their elbows smashed in a cell door if they did not. Christmas was coming, I suggested, hoping that it would give them some ideas. It did, but not the sort that I could relay to the Home Office Honcho. Bloody hell it was cold. My fingers had turned white. I had had more than enough of this lark. Back in the incident caravan I warmed my hands around another cup of tea. No Kit Kat this time.

"Well, Sir, it's Christmas pretty soon and you must know how nostalgic these men get at Christmas, away from hearth and home and so forth. Perhaps if there could be extended visiting over the holiday period. Put up a few decorations perhaps. Maybe have a tree. Put on a panto or a play of some sort. You know, Sir, the sort of things normal people do at this time of year. A chance to count their blessings, a beer or two to toast Her Majesty after Christmas dinner."

"No drink, oh, no, no, no. No drink."

"Yes, Sir, I understand. No drink."

Oh Well it was worth a punt. I was dying for a pint. They would find something to drink regardless. Mr Churchill never let a ready market go without anything.

"Well that sounds reasonably modest er – James."

"I have spoken with the ring leaders, Sir, but that is just a sample of their grievances. Some of the others want their TV replaced and they all want their involvement not to be included on their record when it comes to parole.

"Ringleaders eh? And who are they exactly?"

"Oh Sir, I couldn't really say, not really. If it turned out that I had informed on them, my life would be worthless and I only have a few months to go. As it is there are some men up there who already think that I am your errand boy. Some of these men are, as you know, violent and vindictive men who could if they so wished make my remaining months here sheer hell. Not only that Sir, but some have suggested that there are some screws, er, warders on the take."

In this sort of situation what you don't say is often more important than what you do. For example, I didn't have to say that if someone with an axe to grind should spill the beans to the newspapers about corruption in the prison service then the shit really would hit the fan, big time. They would all get some. The story would run and run. Questions would be asked in the House. Select committees would follow, leaving no stone unturned, witnesses would have to be called. A couple of greedy screws would get it in the neck and be thrown to the wolves. People further up the ladder would be in one hell of a tight spot, regardless of their knowing anything at all. Careers would get put on hold and costs spiral out of control.

Had their skulls been made of Pyrex glass I could not have seen the cogs in their heads whirling with greater clarity.

"Hum, er well, er James. If we can bring this matter to a swift and final conclusion, I can see no reason why we can't make these men's Christmas a little more compassionate and more ..."

"Christian," I said.

"Yes James, and if it were over quickly I could recommend to the Home Secretary that, in the light of possible events, that you were considered for an early..."

"Immediate."

"Immediate release. Yes. I have the authority to sanction that."
I extended a hand which he shook vigorously.

"Well done, well done."

"Well, Sir, I hope that you do not consider me cynical or ungrateful, but could I have that in writing?"

"Yes, I suppose so, um, why not. A hand written note be acceptable?"

"Yes Sir, but you do see my need for caution. I would have to live with these men and already some of them are thinking already that I might be some sort of Judas, a nark, a spy."

"Yes, yes, I can see that, here you are," handing me a hand scribbled note on Prison headed notepaper.

In a borrowed coat and back on the roof, Watts and Gallaway looked within an ace of death.

"OK. Here it is. Mr Churchill will be back in a few days and if things ain't back to normal he will have your balls on a stick for Christmas lunch. Point two is that you two are going to have to take a bit of stick in the short term whatever happens, but if you come down with me now it can only look good for you as reluctant instigators of this little party. That's the bad news. There is some good news and I think all the others ought to hear this and let me know what they think. A crowd gathered in a circle around us.

Christmas is coming and don't ask me how but I have arranged for longer visiting hours, choice of films and lots of other stuff like that. A tree and decorations and a panto. If you want to put one on that is."

"A panto?" says Sparky Watts. "Did he say a bloody panto?"

"Oh yes he did," came the reply.

"Oh no he didn't."

"Oh yes he did," which went on for several minutes.

Sparky said that it was a patronising sop, but his eyes were glowing as if I had promised an orgy with dancing girls.

"Yeah but right now how do you fancy hot showers, dry clobber and chicken soup before lights out. How about it? Who knows Mr C might even come back in a good mood."

Not that I could see that he would if he should return with his trapdoor full of stitches. I for one would not wish to be around here to merit his displeasure. Not that he would have much cause for complaint as far as I was concerned. But you never know what to expect from the likes of him. Egocentric, sociopathic maniacs.

An hour later it was all history. Sap had passed the word to Rasta Johnson's breddrin and everybody, screws included, breathed a collective sigh of relief. Before they filed down the stairway they shouted out "Good old Jimbo. Christmas pudding," or some such nonsense, for puddings, Christmas or otherwise, had never been on the table, so to speak.

Within an hour or two I was outside in the snow looking for a taxi to take me to the nearest pub. I was freezing, I didn't have an overcoat but I didn't give a toss. I was free, with papers to prove it and a few quid in my pocket. All I wanted now to complete my transport to paradise was a fish and chip supper, a couple of large whiskies and a warm bed to continue my dream of Carol Vorderman alone with me on our desert island, and whoever picked up my boot polish, Bic biros and super-soft twin ply toilet rolls was welcome to them with my blessing, for I was a free man looking forward with great expectation to my next big adventure.

THE GREAT KIPPER CAPER

Whistler Williams looked what he was - a shipping clerk. He drove a shipping clerk's car, caught the underground to and from work, ate a shipping clerk's packed lunch and went home to a sweet chunky wife who, you might easily have imagined, had a Plimsoll line tattooed across her plump midriff.

His life, and for him the whole world, was one of precise and predictable order. He had a nice little terraced house. Two immaculately turned out little girls and a minuscule fraction of a timeshare apartment somewhere unpronounceable in Greece. He had life insurance, a pension, ISAs and TESSAs and a few shares in APEX-ZENON LTD, our employer.

Oh yes, in case you are wondering, I have held down a proper job from time to time and if the money at A-Z had only been a bit better I might have walked the straight and narrow for a lot longer, but I digress. All the jigsaw pieces of happiness fitted snugly together. His health was good. The sky as far as the horizon of his imagination would allow was a pristine blue except, as he admitted to himself in his few dull introspective reflections, he was bored to death.

One day he didn't return from lunch, which was strange, and later when he walked into the cellar bar of The Galaxy Club it was stranger still. He wasn't a member of this seedy 24 hours a day drinking establishment. In fact, I was surprised that he even knew of its existence. It was to be a day for surprises.

Already he looked a bit the worse for wear and on his arm Madeline, a lady of the shadows whose looks, virtue and self-respect had come and gone with 1960's optimism. Even at this early hour of the evening he was carrying a greater load than practice or prudence would regard as safe.

"Ah ha," he said.

"What do we have here but Jimbo, my mate, good old Jimbo. Rising star of Apex-Zenon's Buying Department don't you know. Well you should," he added, spraying Madeline's star spangled glasses. This was the sort of uncouth behaviour that she would not normally tolerate from any John, but business had been a bit slack of late and there were younger more adventurous girls arriving from eastern Europe all the time. Not only that, but this was a new customer whose experience of such commerce was limited to films and television and one who, quite understandably, expected well-worn middle-aged street walkers to look the part.

"Here barman."

Eric the bartender scowled at being addressed in such a manner by a stranger, and a drunk stranger at that.

"Here barman. If you please, will you get a drink for my friend Jimbo. A rum and Coke for my, er, friend here and a large scotch for me." Turning to Madeline he added, "Do you know my very good friend, Jimbo? Got me a new carburettor so he did. He will get you a set of gaskets for your moped if anyone can. Get you anything, anything at all. I don't know how he does it, man's a genius, Where 's that drink?"

"Wot you on about? I don't have no bleeding moped. Look you coming back to my place or not? I've a living to make. I can't spend all night..."

"Shush, got to have a drink with Jimbo. Barkeep where's our drinks?"

By this time Eric was getting a bit rattled. If he had to come round the bar, Whistler could expect to be roughly manhandled out into the street where his next steps would in all probability be on all fours along the pavement.

"No more for you pal, You're stewed and in any case not a member, so I couldn't serve you even if I wanted to."

Eric and I go back a very long way. Back to my first brush with the law. Turning to me he said, "This prat really a friend of yours Jimbo?"

I nodded.

"Well, sort of. I never saw him like this before though. Can you call him a cab? Send him home but what his old woman will do to him when he rolls in in this state don't bear thinking about."

Whistler had by this time drifted off into some sort of introspective trance. I gave him a nudge. He awoke with a start. "Save me Jimbo. Save me from drink and the clutches of this harridan harpy."

"Ere what you on about, I don't play no bleeding harp. First it's bleeding mopeds now it's bleeding harps."

"She don't play no bleeding harp," said Whistler laughing uncontrollably at his own little quip the way some drunks will.

"No, you silly old sod, but you will play the harp right enough if Marina catches you in this condition."

"What do I care? What is a woman when all is said and done eh, you tell me that? All bloody hormones, new washing machines and carpets, and, and, and pink slippers."

With that he closed his eyes and fell sound asleep. He wasn't what you would call wide awake as we bundled him into a mini cab and sent him on his way home to Muswell Hill. I lifted his wallet and paid the driver up front. Better that I take charge of it for the weekend than having it make an unsolicited contribution to a Caribbean superannuation fund.

Madeline gave me a look as I did so. A look which said without words that a vacancy had arisen in her early evening social schedule should I be interested in picking up where Whistler left off. Wordlessly I declined and watched as she hobbled up the stairs in a tight leopard skin skirt and stiletto heels which might under other circumstances have attracted the attention of the Health and Safety at Work Executive. Perversely I wondered what her pension arrangements might be like.

I had a couple at the club, two or three in the Kings Arms and another half and half in the Old Market before finding myself outside the front door of the shabby Victorian house where I had a bedsit off of the Paddington Road. Stone cold sober too, which in my book is the waste of an evening and the money it cost.

It was the following Monday after our routine "start the week" departmental conference that I next saw Whistler looking like Marley's ghost trying to forget a bad - Christmas. Over coffee he suggested breaking out of the rat-race once and for all with a little gentle white collar crime, which to me sounded a bit like the Queen's race horse trainer offering to dope the favourite.

As you well know, my career has been a chequerboard of endeavour inside and outside of the restraints of legality so I knew all too well that people turn to crime for any number of reasons, but in a buying department there are already too many temptations to skulduggery. Most of these are very well known to the internal auditors, which is not surprising, these things having been around since Noah's buying clerk put in his first order for bent nails and received an ox and an ass for his trouble. In fact, I understand that a whole term at accountancy night school is devoted to learning the ins and outs of such lucrative ventures as pumping, skimming, loading, trot and double trot. Not to mention bungs and backhanders all of which are far too risky for an old owl to pay any attention to. The risk - reward not being worth the candle. There was no way I was going to throw away the clean record I had built up over the last five years. A-Z knew my record and were good enough to give me a fresh start, and I told him so. Not even for a million quid.

"Yes Jimbo. A million pounds and that's just for starters."

He could see that I was not about to be suckered in.

"I can't do it on my own, Jimbo. I need someone with your knowledge, contacts and experience."

I shook my head slowly and said, although it wasn't completely true, "Sorry Whistler. It's honest Jimbo from now on. It don't pay to break the law," which was true enough. If I were to be tempted from the path of righteousness it would have to be a pretty bloody fool-proof operation, in company with some smart lads who knew their stuff and far beyond the reach of the long arm of the old Bill, but I never told him that.

"That's just it, Jimbo, we wouldn't be breaking any laws, not in England at any rate."

"OK," I said, "let's talk, but not here. If you have so much faith in your plan you can lay out fifty quid and join the Galaxy Club. I will second you and we can talk there."

For a man who services his own car and brings a pack lunch into the office fifty pounds might be a big disincentive. In fact, I was sure it would be, but I was wrong. There he was right on time looking at the pictures in the doorway of the strip club next door.

"Come away you dirty old man, you'll ruin your eyesight," I said, and we made our way down the worn stairs.

If Eric remembered his last visit he didn't say so, took his fifty quid and we both signed in, paid for our drinks and sat down in a quiet corner at the rear.

What he proposed was simplicity itself. We - he and I - buy a few tonnes of say - well anything you like from a long list of commodities, from an EEC country, say England, and export it to a non-EEC country, but one with which we have an open door free trade agreement. As the consignment leaves EEC waters it attracts a rebate from Strasburg. When the ship gets to Nigeria, or wherever, it is turned around re-labelled as a product of that particular third world country, which can then be imported here without having to pay any import duty. Then we re-run the paperwork, and send it round the circle once again. Round and around and around.

We own the export company this end, and the trading company there, so the documentation, invoices, bills offloading etc., are always spot on. "Now Jimbo, here is the cherry on the cake. My uncle Victor is the captain of the MV *Polly Perkins* in the Blue Flash Africa Line so he gets to say what containers are to be unloaded when and where. We have to cut him in for ten percent, but that's fair. In his place I would have wanted a third but even so."

I must have wanted my head examined as I let him talk me into this scam. It all seemed so neat and fool proof. So we did a little trial run and it worked a treat. 500 kilos of cheese went out as genuine Cheddar cheese from genuine Jersey cows, and came back as genuine African goats cheese from genuine African goats.

A year later Mr Black and Mr Green of Luxemburg Overseas Trading visited their bank in Antwerp to check on their bank account. Mr Black - that's Whistler - and Mr Green - that's me - nodded sagely as we were handed our statements and quietly returned by taxi to our hotel where we shocked the receptionist, and the other guests by doing a knees up in the foyer to the tune of *Knees up Mother Brown*.

> *Knees up Mother Brown*
> *Take your knickers down.*
> *Let us see your old fat knees*
> *Lots of dosh from selling cheese.*

All very childish I know but we had over two hundred thousand pounds to split between us after we had paid Uncle Vic his cut. I was never happier to settle an account in all my life.

These days two hundred thousand pounds will just about buy you a flat at the seaside. Back then of course it would have brought us a semi apiece in Pinner, and a new Ford Capri to park in the driveway.

"Listen Whistler," I said over a G&T in the Galaxy Club one night after work. Oh yes, we still kept our jobs. I needed the appearance of respectability if nothing else. Property prices have started to sky rocket and the word "guzzumping" had entered the vocabulary for the first time. I went on to suggest that we quit while we are still ahead.

"With what we have in the kitty we can buy about a dozen cottages in the west country. Some out of the way place like Appledore. Pretty enough but down at heel since the shipyard closed. Do you know what they charge for holiday lets?"

Look at the prices now. I could live the life of Riley on the rents alone, but how could we have known that then? I was still living in a Paddington bedsit, a bigger and more comfortable one, but still a bedsit. I had no wish to attract attention.

Whistler became a bit of a Jeckyl and Hyde character. Starting with a dinner jacket he next gets his teeth fixed by a Harley Street dentist, rents a flat in Mayfair, flies to Monte Carlo over a weekend, drinks champagne till it comes out of his ears, lays the whole bundle on a 50 – 50 shot and doubles our stake. Had he lost it I would have wrung his scrawny neck. Upon his return he buys an Aston Martin, just like the one James Bond drove in *Goldfinger* but without the gadgets, and all the time going home to Marina on the train. It was a wonder that she never noticed when ironing his shirts that the thin Co-Op ones he normally wore had overnight become Jermyn Street's best two-fold cotton.

Still that's women for you and to be fair how might a little butterball from Sidcup be expected to tell a Rolex from a Timex?

Mr Pettigrue, our director, first noticed his hand-lasted Oxfords, and the man from Arthur Anderson the company's external auditors priced his entire turn out in the blink of an eye. Mr Pettigrue took me aside and asked if I had noticed a change in Whistler's behaviour recently. I replied that he had been left some money by an old aunt but I did not know how much, but I thought that it was quite a bit. I should have dissolved our association there and then, but it all went quiet until one day he picks up the wrong briefcase and was on the train before he flicks open the locks and notices, *The Daily Telegraph*, *The Economist* and *Playboy*. All normal enough I suppose, but there in a brown envelope some glossy, half plate, full colour photographs of a big naked lady, old enough to know better. Surely that was ... he caught his breath ... surely not ... but it was ... Mrs Pettigrue.

At the self-same moment, give or take half an hour, in the back of a black cab on his way to a reception at the Institute of Directors, Mr Pettigrue opened what he thought to be his case. There next to the latest copy of *Container Freight Monthly* and the latest copy of *The EEC* rebate review was a letter from Messrs Rolls Royce in Crewe thanking Mr Williams for his order and enclosing a copy of his required specification. If this were not enough the bundle of crisp new £50 notes must have blown his bald head off.

Slowly a light dawned. If he had this case, then his shipping clerk must have his. Oh my god. Full colour photographs of Amelia doing things. Doing things, with things which would have made even poor old Madeline blush.

It was much to his credit that the first thought to percolate up from the deep cracks and crevasses of his mind was *police, I must call the police*. In quick succession other more reflective thoughts followed. What if Amelia found out? What if Wilson had taken copies, and where were they now?

These things can spread like wildfire. The Rotary, the board of A-Z, the private school of which he was a governor, the Conservative Party, the Church and the IoD. The IoD. He must have been speaking out loud.

"Yes governor, the IoD. That's where you wanted to go isn't it?

Well here we are."

He handed the driver a twenty pound note; a ridiculous fee and tip for a journey of just about two miles. In a state of shock he turned and went up the steps. All through that evening his mind was in a blood red torment. If he made his suspicions known about Whistler he could be certain, as sure as God made little green apples, that the photographs of Amelia would be around the firm in an instant, his neighbourhood within days and the Golf Club before, or during, their annual dinner dance, and he would be ruined.

That Amelia might take the children and walk out was paradoxically the last item on his list of concerns. Try as he might, he could not push from his mind the imagined picture of all those leering faces round the boardroom table. God they would see - everything. The picture of the green oriental girl over the bed which he admired so much but was secretly ashamed of. Oh, no, they would see all our special things. Our toys. The fluffy pink bear. The big Barbie doll, Mr Wiggle the elephant that Amelia loved so much, and the little electric gizmo that she loved even more.

Then there was the sombrero that Amelia liked him to wear when they played the rhinoceros game. It was, he concluded, what they call in the movies, a Mexican stand-off. He must pretend to be ill. That's it. She would sense that something was wrong, but he could never tell her. Yes, he must take a few days off work. Go home with a touch of 'flu.

You do not get to be a director of a company like A-Z without having a bit of spunk, and Mr Pettigrue had rediscovered his, as a week later he and Whistler stood face to face over the board room table as they exchanged briefcases.

Was all the money there?

Were all the naughty pictures there?

Had he counted it and made notes of the serial numbers?

Had he taken copies of the photos?

Was the fraud squad on its way?

Were there dozens of stamped addressed envelopes with a trusted friend who awaited a phone call, or the lack of one, before his entire private fantasy world was exposed to the lascivious gaze of polite suburban society.

They both had a lot to lose. They stood there not four feet apart in silence as the perspiration ran in little cold riverlets down their respective spines.

The clock ticked relentlessly onwards. Yet time stood still. Two sets of dentures clicked in dry mouths and two distinct intestinal systems clenched and rumbled with fear. And then, without premeditation, a deal was struck.

I don't know who suggested it first, I only know that I was not consulted and presented afterwards with a fait accompli. We had a new business partner. Green and Black became Green Black and Blue. The little voice at the back of my mind was rolling about chewing the carpet, and screaming at me that now was the time to be intelligent.

Firstly, I had to distance myself from the others.

Secondly, I had to gather and destroy every scrap of evidence linking me to this business, and in case that didn't work as completely as I might have wished, I started to plan how to make it look as if Pettigrue had borrowed my identity for the purpose of his little scam.

With the help of Squidgee Swallowfield, I managed to persuade Whistler to go along with my strategic withdrawal from the enterprise. I don't suppose that you ever met Squidgee, but if you did you would surely remember him for the great ugly scar which ran like a snake across his giant bulldog face. He tells people that he earned it in one of Glasgow's razor gang wars, but I know that he got it mistreating a rotary lawn mower whilst cutting his grandmother's lawn. Still, he looked every inch the frightener lurking at my elbow as I spelt it out to Whistler.

I had no wish for us to part on bad terms, but I had to get it through his thick skull and inflated ego that should everything go pear-shaped, the whole operation was Pettigrue's and I had no part in it at all except perhaps as an innocent. Should he even get wind of Pettigrue putting hands up to any of this and dragging me into the crud with him, let him know that I still had a set of the photographs. A spell inside for fraud might just about be tolerable in the circles within which he moved. Lady Harbinger's Bridge Club, the Conservative Association and so forth but compliance with his wife's visceral shenanigans - never.

As to be expected, without my steady hand at the tiller, when it went wrong, it did. Big time. I will say this for old Pettigrue, he was a sharp bugger. Within three months they had branched out. Not only was there cheese on the menu, but also plums, olive oil, rape seed oil, beef, wine and kippers.

Did I say kippers?

It transpired that for some unaccountable reason the indigenous peoples of the Niger Delta cannot abide smoked fish. In fact, one of their strongest terms of disrespect was "fish eater." Against all their designs a container of the very ripest was actually landed, and after sitting in the hot sun for a couple of days found its way into the interior. Upon arrival at the village on the delivery note, the local witch doctor or public health inspector took one sniff, added a round and fulsome curse to the consignment, and sent it back. Back in their dark steel prison, the entire kipper tribe began to move about to express their mutual discomfort in a most kipper-like fashion. Each day louder and increasingly insistent until their plaintiff cries became more than a little noticeable amid the usual fetid perfumes natural to the docks and jetties, stevedores and labourers of which there are a great number in the coastal regions of the Bight of Benin.

> *Beware, beware The Bight of Benin.*
> *There's one man comes out*
> *If a hundred goes in.*

Or so the old sailors used to say in the days before air conditioning, DDT and Penicillin, and I can see their point. Captain Sven, who had taken on the captaincy of the MV *Polly Perkins* upon Uncle Vic's retirement, had his own particular anodyne for what he amusingly called the bouquet noir, and it came in litre bottles and was called vodka. A bottle a day whilst in any port or anywhere near the equator was guaranteed to hold at bay all manner of evil curses, miasmas, vapours, insects and reptiles, and although not a sensitive soul by nature, was almost, but not quite, prepared for the worst as the big Lascar seaman broke the seal on the container. He puckered his big boxer's nose and said as the big steel door clanged back.

I cannot repeat, much less pronounce, his exact words as they were in Swedish, but you may imagine as well as I the sentiments they contained as a billion Scottish flies weary of sea travel and a monotonous diet rushed out to see what exotic fare the locals had on offer. At the same time a billion African flies in a frenzy resembling the first day of the Harrods sale swarmed in to see what exciting and novel culinary delights might have arrived. Within moments the inter-mixture of this excited crowd blocked out the sun and blanketed the ship, its officers and crew. Captain Sven swiftly locked himself into the wheelhouse and sweated in helpless discomfiture until darkness fell, the land breeze sprang up and the flies called it a day.

Next day as they put to sea on the high tide, Captain Sven ordered the offending container, with its doors firmly closed, to be dumped overboard. Quite naturally everyone who heard about the incident thought the whole thing a hoot. Even more amazingly, what with the rebate and the insurance, it turned a very fair profit. Mr Pettigrue, ever the grand master, had a brain wave. If it could be done with a single container, why not a whole ship load of kippers? If ever there was a time for me to jump ship this was it.

As it happened I had not taken the decision a moment too soon. Even before the World Health Organisation had got to hear of the container of rotting flyblown kippers and the Nigerian authorities had issued a writ for endangering navigation by discarding a container in its territorial waters, Mr Swimbourn of Lloyds was on the case. He was one of the few men in Europe who knew that many Nigerian tribes will refuse to eat fish. They dislike the little bones. All this he kept to himself. He watched and he waited. He prodded and he poked about until he had a file as big as a large suitcase full of evidence, and one ill-fated afternoon met with gentlemen from the serious fraud office who, as is the way with all law enforcement officers, passed the information on to The Metropolitan Police, Customs and Excise and, for all I know, Interpol and M15 as well. One morning not many days later, when the dew was still on the grass they pounced, dragging Whistler away from his buxom wife and Mr Pettigrue from his wife and their favourite toys.

They were both found guilty and both attracted a pretty stiff tariff, but I was kept out of it thank god. I had to admit knowing them both in the early days, of course, but had nothing to do with their business once it was up and running. I even said that I had had my doubts about their activities. I was lucky. I had covered my tracks well enough, and there was no way Whistler would grass. I was looking after his family and his wife at least twice a month.

Mrs Pettigrue lost a whole lot of weight during the trial and it suits her too, and were you to compare the photos in my safe deposit box with the ones I took more recently you would not think that it was the same woman, apart from a fluffy elephant called Mr Wiggle, and the little electric gadget she loves so much.

MERRY CHRISTMAS

I don't care how many times you've heard it before but when
your QC is on his way back to Surbiton in his Lexus and the
judge is wiggling his toes in his carpet slippers and sipping a
Tio Pepe before a blazing fire in his chambers, and the big
metal door bangs shut behind you to the orchestral
accompaniment of jangling keys, the cold hand of panic
clutches at your solar plexus as the grey days, weeks, months
and years in prospect before you extend into infinity. Or five
years, less time served, as the case may be and in my case was.

Five years of sticky dreams of Carol Vorderman. Five years
drooling after a fillet steak and an unquenchable lust for real ale.
Five years marinating in the unforgettable smell of overcooked
cabbage and unwashed feet. Once experienced never, ever
forgotten.

Forgive me if I shudder. The memory is still too recent you see.
Back inside once again thanks to my love for the cutest little girl
in the whole wide world, with the softest baby blue eyes, blond
hair, rosebud lips and a complexion like alabaster. She had a
laugh like tinkling silver bells and the prettiest little turned up
nose you can imagine. Pre-Raphaelite artists would have taken
her to their bosom as the archetypal Dresden porcelain angel.
Ha! I don't believe that you ever met my daughter, Margo. No?

Well, lucky old you.

Not too long ago, I reached the inevitable conclusion that only a right mug continues to work outside the law when he don't have to. Who, in their right mind would wager, at any odds, a regular stroll down to the pub, grilled sole, crème brûlée, expresso coffee and a Remi Martin in a balloon glass against a few grand of flash money followed by endless grey years in some depressing, crumbling Victorian chokey?

Not me, that's for sure. I had had my share of porridge. My mind was set. No kidding. I was going straight from now on. After all, I had a fair bit put away in El Banco de Andalucia, and a nice little holiday villa a few miles inland from the coast. Not earning a fortune mark you, but enough to take care of my little girl. And if I could find the whereabouts of her mother and the garlic chewing Greek cheese vendor she ran off with while I was in the Scrubs, well I had enough to take care of them as well if you catch my drift. Nuff said.

Comfortable, yes that's the word. I was comfortable, so why should I rock the boat with any one of the hundred schemes that invariably come my way. Even when my old mate Harry Hope called around one evening with his maps and Dinky toys I had to turn his proposal down. Although, after a few beers I was tempted because it was a nice, tight, well thought out little operation. The plan in essence was to lift the pre-Christmas takings of John Lewis at Brent Cross. About a million pounds split four ways after deducting 10 % off the top for Mr Churchill, for it goes without saying that he would want his cut of anything going on in his manor.

"Nice of you to offer Harry, I am really flattered and grateful but no. Not this time." And that was that. Sweet sleep favours the just as they say. I slept very well, better than I had for years, secure in the knowledge that the CID would not be calling in the early hours, stomping all over my Kashan rugs and disturbing my domestic routines with impertinent questions and sticking their nosey beaks into things which don't concern them. So I was in excellent fettle at breakfast when I foolishly asked Margot what she would like from Daddy this Christmas. I was feeling pretty safe now that she had passed the gymkhana stage, and pedigree fox-hunters were no longer on her wish list, and was expecting that this year's simply-must-have, would be an iPod, blog, gigabyte, hot-wired, flash, bluetooth or some other piece of fashionable electronic incomprehensibility.

Instead she looks up from her Rice Crispies, all wide eyed and innocent, and says that she wants a Brazilian haircut. Which was fine by me until she told me what it was. Phew. Now there's a career path that wasn't open to me when I left Sprules Road Secondary Modern.

That incurring the half-expected parental wrath, she then asks for a hundred quid in order to have her nose pierced with some piece of tawdry junk and a series of kung fu tattoos on her .... God give me strength. Like she had an interview lined up with a Bombay Brothel and didn't wish to spoil her chances of employment by infringing the house dress code.

Strewth! Give me strength, who'd be a single parent? Now I was just on the cusp of becoming all loud and fatherly and about to splutter … over my dead body … when … ding! A little bell sounded and I had a brainwave. I must confess that I thought that it was one of my best. If I had known then where it would lead I should have let her have every blade of grass mown from the Matto-Grosso, and have allowed her to have a pair of motorcycle handlebars through her cute little nose, complete with brake levers, rear view mirrors, throttle and all, but one never knows you see. The future is a closed book to us all.

Instead, I said, cool and casual as you please, spearing the last bit of fried bread and wiping up the last smear of egg.

"You can have that if you really want my darling. It will make you look like a right tasteless brain dead slag, like all the other tarts pushing prams on a Southwark council estate. But if it makes you happy..."

She was not her father's daughter for nothing and I could see that she sensed that negotiations had not concluded. Her eyes widened a fraction. Some day she is going to make some young man entirely miserable.

Don't push it now Jimbo, I told myself. Pause for effect, "or."

"Or I could buy you - a car."

Whooo Precision bombing or what?

"A car, a Mini, Daddy, a red Mini, really with a C D Player and a Sat-Nav. I must have a hands free kit and lessons of course. The RAC is so much smarter than the AA don't you think? Marcia Wellington will be so jealous. Love you Daddy." Then with a big hug and a kiss she disappeared, texting on her mobile phone as she went.

It was just about, almost, very nearly but not quite worth what happened afterwards to see the pure simple joy that lit up that lovely angelic avaricious little button of a face.

Child psychology! I told myself as I cleared away the breakfast things - piece of cake. I couldn't see for the life of me why parents didn't use it more often. Ah ah! Psychology. The silver key to the golden highway to happiness. Toot, toot or vroom-vroom as Sigmund Freud might have said under similar circumstances. I was, I reflected, getting off rather cheaply with this year's Christmas. Ho Ho Ho.

Wheelie Wilson could get me a banger of sorts from the auction and Clapper McClelland, who was the best driver in the business and owed me big time for keeping him out of the nick by getting the goods on a certain lady magistrate, could teach her to drive. Besides he might think it a hoot to teach a teenager to drive, being unmarried and having no kids of his own to spoil.

Yes, Clapper would help Margot to get her licence, even if he never had one himself, not a real one that is.

Licence or no licence you should see that old boy go when the blue lights on the Jam Sandwich are flashing in the rear view mirror and the big police mouth organ is giving it Toccata and Fugue. He knew short cuts, dodges and wheezes they had not even heard of at the Police Driving School at Hendon.

And for a while that was that. Margot was learning to drive and I was learning to walk the path that is straight and narrow, true to the promise I made to myself.

One Saturday afternoon I had a clear out to test my good resolve and burnt no end of plans and souvenirs in a dustbin in the back garden. Including in the smoking pyre, a very educational stack of photographs of a certain lady magistrate au-natural, or au-unnatural to be strictly accurate. My word, what they get up to in Carshalton.

I had just covered the lot with a wad of dead leaves and rose clippings, and listening for the sound of a new page being turned in the book of life when a Ford Scorpio pulls up outside burbling like a Ferrari, out from which pops Clapper with a toothy grin, all washed, brushed, booted and suited.

"What ho, Clapper?" says I. "You'll get my vote if you're standing for parliament. I'll vote for anyone brave enough to wear brown brogues with a light blue suit and a red kipper tie. Odd socks too, very innovative."

In what must have been an entrenched nervous habit he stood on one leg and polished a shoe on the back of his trouser leg whilst twisting his pork pie hat between his large hands.

"Er, Jimbo," he stuttered.

"Yes Clapper?"

"Er, Jimbo."

"Yes you said that once. What's up? You on the cadge? Has Margot run over a copper in your car? Smart girl – no? Well?"
"Margot – yes," he said at last.

His Pork Pie hat couldn't take much more punishment. Already the band had come off. All eighteen stone of him was trembling. No wonder he became a get-away driver; he could never have run away.

Under not too dissimilar circumstances a primary school teacher might have said Clarence McClellan go and sit on the silly stool in the corner until you have calmed down. I couldn't say that, of course, so I said the next best thing.

"Fancy a beer?"

"No, no this is too important."

I was all ears. "Yes. well better spit it out then, Christmas is coming."

"I, er, we, er, love one another - and I have come here today, Sir, to ask for your daughter's hand in marriage."

He gave his hat a final twist and looked at his shoes. Where on earth did an oaf like Clapper get a phrase like that? Some re-hab course back in the day I suppose. Borstal like as not.

This was too much to take in all at once. Clapper McClellan wishing to call me Daddy. This same Clapper who picked his teeth with a fork and trimmed his toenails with a razor blade. The same Clapper I had taught to read the *Beano* whilst on remand, calling me 'Sir' and asking for hands. It didn't bear thinking about. He was ten years older than me for crying out loud.

Still when ASBO Cupid's little arrow catches an old lag in the eye it's a case of GBH and no mistake.

I wanted to laugh out loud when I thought of Clapper hanging out with all the dudes in Margot's set at the end of term disco, complete with silly woollen hat, skateboard and ... Oh God, stop it before I have a fit or something. Clapper McClellan giving up his souped up Scorpio for a BMX bike. To this day I do not know how I stopped myself from rolling about on the damp lawn screaming fit to bust, but I held it in until he left.

I told him that I would have to consult Margot's mother (wherever she was holed up). As I heard him pull away it was all I could do to hold a tin of beer. It frothed up and went all over the place. Every time I calmed down a bit enough to take a swig, I could see this great lout doing wheelies and bunny hops on this little BMX bicycle, and almost choked. Doing the Macarena, the Salsa and bopping the night away totally off his pudding on E or LSD, loving up all the brothers and sisters in the crush.

Nice baggies, cool trainers, respects mi man. Some of the Gangsta Coons round here would be in for a surprise if they came the old acid with Clapper. Now that would be something I would buy a ticket to see.

It was all tosh anyway, Margo had no romantic interest in him at all or, for that matter, having any further lessons with him.

She could not quite make him see that the driving examination conducted under the auspices of the Ministry of Transport tended to look for competence in hill starts, not racing starts, from outside Barclays in the High Street. Three point turns were de rigeur whereas handbrake turns were not.   Quite sensibly Margot recognised it for what it was. A middle aged man's infatuation. So that was all right, wasn't it?

No it wasn't all right, and that she might as well tell me now as later. My heart sank. She intended to quit school after Christmas and leave home. It wasn't healthy for a girl of her age to live alone with a man of my age. Her father mark you.

"But where will you go?" I asked, images of rat infested hippy squats in derelict buildings forming in my mind

"It's all right Daddy. Miss Hutton, my arts teacher, says that I can have her spare room and instead of paying rent I could perhaps model for her."

I bet she could. I knew all about M's Hutton. I knew all about 1960's Sappho love children run to seed. I had seen Judy Dench's *Notes to a Scandal*. This child would be the death of me, and they say single mothers have it tough.

It was a programme on BBC 2 which gave me a way out and planted the idea of a Swiss Finishing School in my febrile mind. A few terms learning Cordon Bleu cookery and walking up and down long flights of stairs in high heels with big, serious books balanced upon her head and she would emerge like a butterfly from its cocoon, all recollection of Clapper forgotten and all thoughts of butch arts teachers irrevocably erased. A suitable bride for a Duke or an Earl, or even a judge. Now there's a thought.

Unfortunately, I had sold her on the idea of blue skies, gluhwein and unlimited year round skiing (artificial snow if necessary) before I had reckoned the cost. Hell's teeth, they call us thieves. I could have run a Lear Jet for less and joined the Athenaeum with the change. There was only one thing to do - curse it. I had to go back to work.

The job went like clockwork. A cuckoo clock as it turned out, as four men dressed in Santa suits quietly relieved the John Lewis Partnership of over a million quid.

Harry Hope and his minder, the gigantic Simon Smaill, both back in civvies, hopped out at Lancaster Gate tube station and were never seen again, Clapper put his foot down and left twin streaks of burnt rubber along Bayswater Road as he raced off.

"Here slow down, Clapper," I said. "We don't want to attract attention, do we?"

Still he drove faster, and faster still. A wheel trim flew off at Marble Arch. A pedestrian shouted something anatomically impossible and two traffic cops looked up like synchronised puppets, and their large gleaming white BMW motorcycles burst into life.

"Oh Christ," I said. "Here, let me out here, Clapper. Now."

"Ruined - ruined - my life is ruined," he said with a sob, which was half groan.

"How could you be so cruel - so heartless - you - you fiend."

This was a new Clapper.

"You are sending my dear little Pippet away, and now my heart is broken and you will not get away with it you unfeeling brute."

With a clarity born of a profound fear of imminent arrest, I realised that by some mysterious evolutionary path of personal development Clapper had graduated in a single gigantic bound from the *Beano* as literature of choice, and in an unexpected renaissance of spirit had discovered the exemplary paradigm espoused in Messrs Mills and Boon's excellent works of romantic fiction.

"Now, look here Clapper - it's not what you think. If you will slow down just a bit l will try to explain."

"If I slow down you'll run away."

Well he wasn't as stupid as all that. We were racing down the Mall now.

60 - 70 - 80. My God he was going to attract the attention of every cop in A division at this rate.

"Look, Clapper, if you want her hand, she's yours. I was only acting for the best. She is so very young don't you see. If you love her as you say you do surely you can wait a bit. Say till the end of term. What do you say old pal? Start again. Let's be friends. What. Come on, for old time's sake. Take it easy eh."

His eyes bulged with fury, and his lips were set with firm resolution.

"For Christ's sake stop you crazy fat old bastard, you're going to get us killed."

"Yes," he said

Oh mother, oh my, Oh! Sweet Jesus, No, oh my God, he really wants to kill us both.

Wonderful thing radio. The two traffic cops who had clocked us at Marble Arch weren't going to get their nice new white motorcycles anywhere in the way of over a ton of hot motorcar driven by nearly a ton of a star-crossed lunatic in love. Instead they organised a gang of far more expendable pedestrian plod, who set up a road block, while, like the sensible fellows which they were, hung back to watch the fun.

Clapper kicked down and the engine roared an excited and angry bellow as he headed for the central car. I assumed the foetal position, gritted my teeth and prayed. I prayed that they would assume that I was an innocent hitch hiker. They didn't.

"If I can't have her no one shall," were his somewhat illogical last words as he went head first through the windscreen until only his brightly polished brogues and odd socks remained inside the car resting at unnatural angles upon the steering wheel. In his murderous and suicidal anger, Clapper had failed to notice that I was wearing a seat belt and had a large holdall full of used banknotes, a Santa suit and a false beard on my lap, not to mention a stuffed Rudolph the reindeer who, with an expression of Scandinavian aplomb, regarded the whole outing as a bit of a lark. A rich eccentric hitch hiker then. No. Not much of an excuse much less a defence.

My head was spinning with thoughts of gay art mistresses and facial tattoos. I thought at first they were singing Once in Royal David's City, but it was only the old mantra. You need not say anything unless you wish to do so as bank notes swirled and gathered in the gutter like huge green snowflakes.

I didn't have to say anything, but I did. In fact, I blabbed.

"No, no, no. Not me, Clapper was driving, He's in love you see. And then there's the artificial snow, that costs extra don't you know. Every bloody thing costs extra at the bloody Ecole DuPont. I didn't have a choice. It was either the Cordon Bleu lessons or the Bombay brothel. If you have children, you will understand officer. That's why I am going straight. For my little girl. Selfish bitch. You must understand. That's why I am going straight you see. Straight as an arrow. Straight is the path and narrow is the gate. It says that in the Bible. You really must read the Bible. It's a great comfort in times of trial. Yes, there will be a trial I suppose."

I could hear myself slurring these idiotic words as if from a great distance and could sense darkness closing in as my legs turned to jelly.

"Ooops Santa, let go of Rudolph. Take his arm George, get him in the van. Mind his head."

It started to snow.

"It's not fair, because I have to go straight."

"Easy now, Santa, we'll see you go straight. Won't we boys?"

Yes, Sarge. Straight to prison.

Ho Ho Bloody Ho - Merry Christmas.

LITERARY C⊕NSEQUENCES

You might well ask. You might very well ask. How a man with serious literary aspirations, a love of books and reading can find himself sitting here in the dark surrounded by fifty ton of coke in boiler house number one beneath the beetling grey Victorian walls of one of Her Majesty's middle ranking penal institutions.

Of water I have lots from a brass spigot on the boiler. Not Evian perhaps, but it serves its purpose. Of food I have none. The big bag of pork scratchings and the Mars Bar I brought with me are long gone. If I could find a mouse I would eat it raw. At least it isn't cold.

Do you write at all? I suspect that you do, but let me tell you, brothers and sisters of the Bic Biro, that it is because of the self-same phantom appeal of literary pretentious that you find me in this predicament. Cowering down here with the spiders, in fear for my life. What sort of career option is it at this crossroad of my time on this planet, which offers slow starvation on the one hand, and a bloody good kicking on the other?

The screws think that I have gone over the wall, taking all prospect of an early release with me. Mr Churchill, the head villain in here, thinks that I intentionally have made him out to be a right plonker. Never my intention of course, not that that matters a snuff. God help me. I am in for some evil stick either way.

I tell you it don't pay to be too nice.

A couple of months ago I was propped up on pillows in the hospital wing where I was recovering from having had a wart removed.

Don't you dare bloody well laugh. It was about this big, painful and in a very embarrassing place. I was still sore, but extremely relieved to be shot of it. With peace and quiet and slightly better food it was quite a little holiday, and I just lay there reading. Oh, I don't know what exactly, just some American crap about white hunters in Africa, thick natives with big bundles on their heads, lions, ivory and society women with expensive tastes. You know the sort of thing as portrayed by Stewart Granger at the pictures. Suddenly Mouse Morgan sidles up alongside, lethargically pushing a huge floor duster.

"Cor, what's that all about, Jimbo?" he says with eyes on stalks at the picture of the busty blonde on the front cover in need of a perm, and about to be ravished by a lion while some big black bloke loiters about in the background leaning on his spear and looking too smug by half. I started to read him a bit, just a paragraph or two and would you believe it, next day even before they had changed the dressing on that tender spot, Mouse was back and with him Bongo the regular ward orderly, and a new bloke called Twicely. Don't ask.

Bloody cheek I thought, but it turns out that almost half the mugs in here can't read or write. Now isn't that an indictment on the low life that run our country. Well, Britain has to come top in something I suppose even if it's only ignorance.

So to cut a long story short, by the time I had all my amenities restored and in full working order I had about a dozen, mostly old geezers, sitting on the edge of my bed and that of Boots Burnside my cell mate hanging onto my every word, or waiting outside on the landing for the next instalment of whatever it was I happened to be reading at the time. It was like listen with mother, or feeding time at a trout farm; all wide eyes and open mouths. Enough to make you want to throw up? I should say so, but it was flattering too in a way to be the centre of so much rapt attention. Even so I was getting fed up with it.

"OK chaps," I said, or words to that effect. "What if I taught you to read? And then you can get your own books out of the prison library and read the dirty bits over and over again if you want!"

Well they liked the idea of that, and so did Mr Porter - the new Deputy Chief Warden - who came up with a whole lot of books and supporting material. All of which had to look good on my record.

Sadly, my first lesson was also my last. Peter the Greek took one look at the course book, threw it across the room and in the thickest Glasgow accent expressed the consensus of the assembled class, and thus condemned the whole project.

"Is ya takin tha piss or wha? This shite is fa bairns an I ant avin any of it."

And I for one could see that he had a point.

John has Blue shoes,
Jane has Red shoes.

It was all a bit too infantile to be taken seriously by the kind of students we had in here. Funny thing is, they took their books back to their cells with them.

Jane did have nice legs and John's shorts - well you don't need to be Sigmund Freud to work that one out in a place that has more perverts to the square yard than the House of Lords and The Groucho Club combined.

Dejected but relieved that the whole episode was over, I collected my cocoa and went back to my cell and my new paperback who dunnit, *Lady don't fall backwards*.

I had just got into the first colourful page when my cell-mate, young Frank Wetherby, who was just trying out a five year stretch to see if he likes the life, having got wind of how the class went, starts up a conversation.

"Thing is Jimbo," he said with uninvited familiarity and offering me one of his Jaffa Cakes. "It's all written for kids innit? They won't wear that. Thick they may be, but they have their pride."

I thanked him for the Jaffa Cake, and went back to my book, but I couldn't get back into it. That's the problem with having an over-active imagination. I couldn't let the matter rest.

What was needed here was something simple, but not condescending. Something in the lingua-franca of the underworld. Stories they could relate to. I let my mind dwell on it until the lights went out. Oh sod it I had forgotten to brush my teeth. Next day, having not much to do, I got a few ideas down on paper and ran the concept past Dark Wellington, the nearest thing to a backward child to hand. He sat down quietly, all ears as I gave him a few sample sentences.

"Badger is tooled up."

"The get-away car is ready."

"This is a stick up," said Toad.

"Who is the grass?" asked Ratty.

Badger's moll is wearing high heels and after the blag she is going to give him a great big...

OK perhaps not that bit. Better save that sort of thing for the advanced class.

Dark Wellington was hopping up and down on his chair with excitement.

"Cor, cool, Jimbo, real cool, can't wait for the next instalment to see if they get away with the stick up or if some slag has grassed them up to the old bill. Is Badger's moll going to give him the works when he gets back to their drum? What sort of shooter was it? A sawn off shotgun, yeh that's best. Scare the crap out of the old git behind the counter. Put a couple into the ceiling for effect. That's what I would do."

Talk about reading between the lines. Next thing he was telling me where the gang could get a hot BMW with false plates. So much for market research. The thing is if you have a mind like mine the ideas and the scams come so thick and fast that within a couple of days my dreams of becoming author-publisher to the illiterate incarcerated were all but forgotten.

About a week later I was bartering a PP3 battery and a tube of toothpaste for a half bottle of Night Nurse which I hoped to trade for Old Holborn with Dopey Desmond, who somehow manages to inject the stuff, when a little scroat called Pecker Wood casually passed the word.

When you have the unquestioned authority of Mr Churchill in this nick you do not send out written invitations. You do not even need to send a henchman to deliver the invite by hand, unless it's urgent that is. All you really need to do is to say, ever

so softly, "Tell Jimbo that I should like to see him – now."
Which means hang on to your fruit salad, it's serious. But if it
should be "Be so kind as to ask Jimbo to call at his earliest
convenience," it is Omah gawd! What's he want me for now-
trouble. Time to fold a hand towel into a neat square and wrap it
around the old family jewels. Thus you see how the word is
passed from the highest to the lowest.

With trembling fingers, I knocked softly on Mr Churchill's cell
door.

"Come in Jimbo, come in," said Mr Churchill looking very
smart in his Saville Row tailored prison uniform. Laying aside
his worn Penguin copy of *À la recherche du temps perdu*, and
setting down his glass of dry sherry, "Have you ever read
Proust, Jimbo?"

"Er, no- not yet. Always meant to but er..."

"Very esoteric Proust, arcane even. Yes. Not for everyone-in
here - hum."

And for a moment his privileged position and his luxury cell
failed to bring him solace and a thunder cloud rolled across his
ignoble lined brow.

"Yes," he said with a sigh looking up, "and temps don't get
much more bleeding perdu than in here, do they?"

I coughed softly to remind him of my presence, and he suddenly
found himself back on earth amid familiar surroundings.

"Er - I believe you wished to see me Mr Churchill," I said.

"Please, Jimbo, where are my manners, take a seat, no not there,
take the comfy one - have a piece of Turkish Delight."

Oh shit, now I was in for it. Mr Churchill gets what he wants, when he wants it. He doesn't need to be cordial to draw you into his little plans. Plans which usually result in somebody getting dumped upon and all too frequently it is me.

"Jimbo, relax, you look so tense, is it the presence of the boys?"

"Boys scram." They scrammed.

Did I ever introduce you to any of Mr Churchill's boys? The executive arm of his fiefdom, now there's a play on words for you.

The old one with the dashing facial scar and a neck like an elephant's leg is Nethaniel Bone. Don't ever call him bone head or Neanderthal Bone. Not if you value the integrity of your bones that is. The other was Grinder Mills, standing in for Bread Knife Baker, currently in London on display at the Old Bailey. Ah, oh I mustn't forget the third man of the hour. Hopalong Hopkins. I knew him when he was just plain Harry Hopkins before he fell out with one of Rasta Johnson's boys over a matter of racial theory.

Old Bone was OK. I quite liked Old Bone. He reminded me of another South London heavy, my Uncle George, to whom he bore a striking resemblance. The best thing about Bone was that he was susceptible to reason. Well, not reasoned with exactly, that's silly. Bought would be a better word. If it did not conflict with what he considered to be his duty to "der boss". Very ethical I'm sure. I sometimes slipped him a Curly-Wurly, a favourite of his at the time, just to keep him friendly like. If he had to "do you" then an ounce of Old Holborn would mean blood and bruises instead of ruptures, broken bones and teeth. Cheap insurance for there was no knowing when Mr Churchill might want to make an example of one of his flock.

Grinder was a different kettle of cold fish. Overtures of intimate friendship are not to be recommended in that direction. For apart from being a sadistic muscle-bound killer serving a life sentence, Grinder is as queer as a house proud cockroach. God help any baby-faced, young tearaway who crosses his path in here. He would have something torn away all right.

Never mind all your ASBOs and community punishment. A short honeymoon in a lock up with Grinder would put anybody off a life of crime. Well, how would you like your eyes poked out from the south-west. Urgh, don't bear thinking about. There is a little cell at the end of a landing in B Wing where they put all the younger offenders the guards consider to be at risk. It has a coffee coloured door.

Grinder calls it his chocolate box and since his taste these days favours the liquorice ones and the little brown ones with soft centres, no one minds too much, and a collective sigh of relief is breathed by all. But I digress.

I declined the proffered Turkish Delight, real oriental stuff not the mass produced stuff, full of eastern promise.

"Now Jimbo, about this novel you are writing."

"Actually it's not a novel Mr G, it's a ..."

"Don't be modest, Jimbo. Us writers must stick together in adversity beneath this little tent of blue which we call the sky. Now tell me all about it. I've had a synopsis from Kenny Keys, who is very buddy-buddy with young Frank Wellington. The armed robbery goes astray. The grass gets his comeuppance when the moll Alice gets him in the throat with a stiletto, and they dump his body in a Diggerland Theme Park. We can call it "Alice's Adventures in Diggerland.""

I wanted to tell him that it wasn't a novel at all, just a silly idea for a remedial reading primer and I hadn't actually written a word, but only a right mug would try to stop him in full flow with his boys just outside.

"As I see it Jimbo, it is about this highly intelligent good looking chap from ... Oh could be anywhere, but let's say Camberwell."

"That's where you come from, isn't it Mr Churchill?"

"So it is Jimbo - I hadn't realised that. Well this chap, genius that he undoubtedly is, can't get a decent chance from the system and so he turns, after much soul searching, to a life of crime in order to support his poor old crippled mother."

I suddenly remembered a story told to me by my Uncle George about old Mrs Churchill breaking into warehouses during the blackout and beating up any copper foolish enough to be out and about during an air raid.

"You might put in some stuff about how he had to be strong and single minded to survive in those austere days down the Walworth Road. Add in some good action, punch ups with the Flying Squad. Not forgetting two faced corrupt cops on the take. You might even call one of them DS Robert Preston of M Division."

"Sorry but isn't he a real..."

"Don't interrupt Jimbo, I ain't got all day. For colour add in some good deeds and don't forget to mention his rich and varied love life. I will leave it to you to fill in the hack work, so let's cut to the denouement as we writers say. One day whilst working in the governor's garden he meets, quite by chance the governor's new bride. Let's call her Cora. Their eyes meet and

'Bingo'. It was love at first sight. She aids his escape and together they nick a rich Arab's motor yacht which has a safe just full of dosh, gold, diamonds and stuff like that and hi ho, off they go to start a new life together in Rio. You could add that the randy bitch can't get enough of me, er, I mean him, even when they stop off for group sex on a millionaire's tropical Seychelles island in the South Pacific. Worn to a frazzle I, er, he still manages to .... What is it Bone? Can't you see I'm busy?"

"Two o'clock boss."

"Sorry Jimbo, must end it there, must phone my broker in New York. Bring me the first chapter by Monday."

He didn't actually say "Or Else" but he might have done. I walked back to my cell utterly amazed. Not by the way he believed that the creative process worked, nor by his lack of geographical knowledge, but by the fact that with all the latest weather girls to fantasize about, not to mention Carol Vorderman, he should entertain lurid and lascivious thoughts about Crab Apple Cora, the governor's wife. It left me speculating what it was they were putting in his cocoa. I scribbled a few pages over the next couple of days, but my heart wasn't in it. Then I had a brain wave, one of my best, or so I thought at the time.

I pinched an edition of a Mills and Boon romance from the library. You would be amazed at the varied literature available to inmates in a modern prison. Read it through a couple of times to get the feel of the thing. Borrowed a portable typewriter and settled down to produce my opus magnum. I changed the setting from Cairo to Camberwell of course. Changed the part where he rescues his beloved from where she was being held captive by Tureq rag heads by the oil wells in the desert, to their escape from toe-rag skinheads in Dalston to the safety of Tunbridge Wells. I changed the Casbah to Petticoat lane, the French

Foreign Legion to the Old Bill and all the hard work was done. Mr Churchill fair lapped it up but couldn't for the life of him see why they had made good their escape on a camel.

Well I had to make a few mistakes somewhere but not as blatant as that.

"Does it say camel Mr Churchill? Typing error. That should be they made good their escape in a Scammel, you know, a big British Leyland lorry. Then calamity struck. I mean how was I to know that he meant to get the bloody thing published, and by sending it to Messrs Mills and Boon for starters.

The funny thing was that they accepted it at face value at first, and sent Mr Churchill a contract and a substantial cheque. To him you note, not me, and then some busybody of a proof reader goes sucking up to the boss and says something like, "Excuse me Sir, but that new book *Races for Love* by Clarence Churchill, is really our book *Oasis of Love* by Mrs Audrey Pengellis, with extra violence, sex and four letter words. Oh yes sir, certain, do you think we should prosecute?"

Well thankfully they declined that option. Didn't want the adverse publicity I suppose, but they stopped the cheque which he had had framed as a trophy on his wall.

I suppose that I might have escaped with a bloody good slap if I had brazened it out there and then, but I kept shtum.

And when the secret did get out, as secrets will, and Mr Churchill discovered that I had modelled him as the hero in the original *Oasis of Love* who - in the story - turns out to be some big black character, E Wing was in uproar, with his arch rival Rasta Johnson rolling about laughing. "Invitin' 'im ta come over to chew da fat wid I an' de bredrin 'n' light up da fire an burn some erb."

By this time there was a price on my head, and I was a wanted man. Bone and Grinder put out the word that news of my whereabouts would be rewarded with a two-ounce tin of choice and they also let it be known that anyone assisting my evasion could expect a negative reward, unless of course they already had more fingers than they knew what to do with and would like to be divested of their excess stock.

So here I am in the dark sitting on the boiler-house coke with my empty bowels churning fit to burst with terror awaiting the *auto-da-fé* which must surely follow at some stage. No food in prospect and the duty stoker expected at any moment.

The door to the boiler room creaked, lowering the temperature of my blood several degrees. Backlit from the light in the stairwell, two basilisk-like silhouettes paused at the top of the concrete steps. My pulse pounded in my ears. "Hello Bone, Grinder. Fancy meeting you here. Is there something I can do for you?"

A NEW LEAF

Two men of old school military aspect with closely cropped silver hair stood talking inside the gatehouse of Her Majesty's Prison - Greywall - in the County of Yorkshire, waiting for the kettle to boil on the electric ring. One wore the dark blue uniform of the prison service, the other dressed in a comfortable well-worn tweed jacket, the sort seldom seen these days with leather patches on the elbows.

"Well, Stanley how does it feel to be retiring from the service after, what, twenty years is it?"

"Yes, Barney, twenty-two years in the civilian service and another ten with the military police at Colchester Barracks before that. I've handed over my keys for the last time. Just popped in for one last cup of tea, say goodbye to the lads, and see which of our customers is being let loose at the same time."

"Let's see," said Barney picking up a clipboard.

"This will be a computer screen soon, but I shan't have to worry about that, my contract will be up in a few months and I shall get as far away from this place as fast as my legs will carry me. What have we got here? Phillips B the kiddie fancier, never thought that he would get out alive. Evans P, Evans S, Jones T, and an old customer Three Fingers Bone N. The enforcer. How will Mr Churchill manage without him?"

"He'll be back inside of a month you mark my words. Some of them can't make it out there in the real world and end up back in here where they feel safe you'll see."

"Here's an old regular coming down the stairs now. From what I hear he is determined never to do any more time. William James, your very own Jimbo. You and he go back a fair old way I believe."

"Yes, I was on duty here when he came in for the very first time. He wasn't much more than a kid then; criminality is written into that man's genetic material like Brighton in a stick of rock. For all his smart-arsed chat he is as rotten as the rest of them. So crooked he could eat nails and shit corkscrews. He'll never change. Mind you the last five years has aged him. Another stretch like that and he will die inside. Even in a nice new suit with shoes brightly polished, release papers and travel warrant in his hot sticky little hand he is still a thief"

"Mr East, Mr Soaper, well here we all are ready to take the world by storm."

"That'll be the day, Jimbo, when a shower like you will raise a storm. Got your next bit of villainy planned yet have you?"

"Steady on Mr East, as of 12 o'clock it's Mr James to you. Society and I are quits. Believe it or not I am going to go straight this time, honest."

"Go straight Jimbo? You couldn't go straight with a spirit level up your jacksie."

"That's a bit unkind Mr Soaper. Seriously though, I have had enough of these places to last me several lifetimes. I've a bedsit sorted out, and an interview for a job lined up driving a mini cab. So if you would be so kind as to open up the sally port I will be on my way. I do have a train to catch you know."

"Sally port, what are you on about?"

"A sally port is that little door set in the main gate. From the old French you know."

"Yeah, yeah, still the smart arse. On your way sunshine. See you soon."

"Aren't you going to wish me luck Mr East, Mr Soaper"

"Jimbo, just piss off. You'll be back in no time flat."

The door closed behind him with a satisfactory clunk. The sky was blue. There was a hint of autumn in the air, fallen leaves and wood-smoke. Somewhere in his heart great flocks of songbirds awoke and gave voice as he walked the half a mile to the railway station.

Back in the gatehouse the kettle boiled and the tea brewed.

"So what is it to be Stanley, golf or roses?"

"First things first, Barney. I am going down to London to pay my daughter a visit and then I am going to take the grandchildren off her hands for a few weeks and take them to visit Disneyland for a nice long holiday. Ever since her husband Paul died she has had a lot on her plate, poor little bitch. Keeping the garage running and looking after the kids. If London wasn't so far away I might have done more to help, but I am determined to make it up to her.

"A few weeks on her own might give her a chance to sort herself out and perhaps find herself a nice steady chap to be a real father to those children. I've said as much. Look here my girl I said, you're still a good looking woman and you're smart too. Ever since she was a nipper she always had her nose in a book. Got that from her mother. She could take her pick. Accountant, doctor or even a dentist, they make good money these days. But not another mechanic, another grease monkey. Paul was a good lad I suppose, but a bit thick. Thick enough to be under a lorry without supports when the jack failed. Spread your net a bit wider this time my girl. You can do it. And do you know what she did? She laughed and kissed me. Said I was an old fuss pot that's what."

The Florida sunshine was fantastic and his daily dip in the ocean quickly washed away the prison odour as the sun turned his grey lined face to crimson and dried up that miasma which marks a man whose life is spent behind windowless walls in the company of men who might explode in a fit of violence at any moment.

His first real hamburger and his first pint of frothy ice cold American beer had been a refreshing novelty to begin with, but within a week he was starting to itch for some real ale.

Young's Special or Fuller's ESB for choice, although Theakston's would serve equally well. After ten days it became a craving exacerbated by visions of a Sunday roast with Yorkshire pudding and lashings of gravy, and real mustard - not the sweet tasteless yellow muck they serve over there.

They had sampled all the rides, seen all the alligators and dolphins and parrots and were in that wind down stage of a holiday in the final week when you start packing, buying presents for relatives and friends and books for the long flight home. From out of nowhere he suddenly remembered that it was Wednesday.

Wednesday was always curry day in the prison. His mouth watered at the very thought. Unsophisticated as it was, he could even smell it now and wondered if Jimbo, at this moment, was also feeling the need for a curry. He dismissed the thought. Why on earth should he care what Jimbo was having for lunch? He could see him now before his mind's eye in his sordid little bedsit off the Wallworth Road, eating a takeaway chicken korma with a plastic spoon from a foil container. Some habits are harder to break than others, and so a chicken korma was unintentionally added to his epicurean wish list.

There are few things more reassuring to the long haul air traveller than the cool, well-modulated tones of an English pilot calling from the flight deck, "The time in London is 1800 hours, it rained on and off all day with further showers expected later. The temperature is 9 degrees and the wind gusty." Etc., etc., so on and so forth.

Outside the terminal building they waited in a very British orderly queue for a taxi. At last a smart black Vauxhall drew alongside with rain sitting in bright glassy beads on its new paintwork.

With the luggage and the children safely aboard he looked at the driver for the first time in any detail. In actual fact he stared fixedly at the back of the man's head. There was something very odd about the driver's left ear. It had a series of V shaped notches cut into it. He knew that ear. He knew the man in possession of such an organ and he also knew how it came to be figured in such a fashion.

Three Fingers Bone had put it there with a pair of heavy duty toe nail clippers at the behest of Mr Clarence Churchill as a demonstration to the other inmates that bad faith in the matter of unpaid interest on quite small loans would not be tolerated, and that no part of an offender's anatomy would be held sacrosanct on purely sentimental grounds if, for reasons of his amour-propre, the status-quo needs must be maintained and actions of a punitive nature are considered to be not just necessary, but essential. But this extraordinary punishment was not inflicted over the mere repayment of a little loan, but to settle a dispute over the authorship of some book or other. He never did find out the true story. Mr Churchill was in high dudgeon for weeks, and of course discipline suffered accordingly, for there was an unspoken alliance between the authorities and the senior villain to keep things quiet. A febrile atmosphere adversely affected the day to day business of everyone concerned, a situation to be deplored and avoided at all costs.

But it couldn't be. But it was. Just when he thought that all reminders of his working life were behind him, here it was back to haunt him in three dimensions.

"Jimbo," he said, somewhat louder than he intended.

"Good holiday Mr Soaper?"

He regained his equilibrium really rather quickly.

"Oh yes James and how is your life progressing? I can see that you are working. Settling into your bedsit OK are we?" He could not keep the edge of sardonic bitterness out of his voice as pictures of how he imagined Jimbo's small, cramped, uncomfortable, tatty pied-a-terre sprang to mind. A little like a prison cell, but with curtains and without the bars.

"Better than well, Mr Soaper, a whole lot better than well. As you see I have a regular job and a regular girlfriend."

There was something like joy and excitement in his voice. The need to tell a friend, or in fact anyone, of his conversion to the world of simple mundane happiness.

"From the moment we met I knew in my heart that my future prospects were looking bright. Married before of course but that's the way things are these days. Couple of kids too, and a stuffy old grandad she is going to have to look after sooner or later."

"Congratulations, Jimbo," he said, only half meaning it.

"When's the happy day?"

"Don't know the answer to that one, but I have asked her. Just last night in fact and again in the early hours of this morning and she said that she was going to think about it."

The traffic lights changed to red, and the taxi slowed to a halt.

"Poor cow," he thought, "shackled to this one." But he said nothing, and then as one thing followed another there were other thoughts. More a series of pictures than thoughts. Some twice around the block South London bimbo. All big tits, short skirts and high heels. What a distraction that would make on visiting day in the nick. But he wouldn't be there to see it as he had to remind himself. The lights changed back to green, and the big Vauxhall moved off swiftly, eating up the miles.

"That's it, take the third left off the high street just past Boots the chemist, then next right and second left. Pull up by the monkey puzzle tree. Just here."

The taxi pulled up rather abruptly, decanted the passengers and suitcases in something of a rush. The driver looking up and down the street furtively as if he didn't want to be seen.

"How much do I owe you James?" he said reaching for his wallet.

"Er, nothing, nothing at all Mr Soaper. This one's on me. On the house, water under the bridge, may old acquaintance be forgot. Yes, that's it. Must dash, another fare to collect, round the corner in Sunshine Gardens. Must be off ."

The former prison officer was exhausted. Too jet-lagged to reflect for long on this sudden gesture of friendship and generosity, for the front door was soon opened to a forest of arms and a barrage of hugs and kisses. "Welcome home dad."

Over a cup of real tea in her warm kitchen she could not contain the excitement, which was clearly evident in her sparkling eyes, which he might have noticed earlier had he been alert enough and less jet lagged. The girls started an argument as overtired children will, as to who should use the telephone first to phone their school friends with stories, mostly made up, about their romantic encounters with surfing dudes on the beach.

"Girls, please be quiet for a moment. I have something important to tell you, you and Daddy that is."

The pause was, as they say, pregnant and he certainly hoped that she wasn't.

"I'm engaged to be married."

The girls took the news better than she imagined, but with no ebullient enthusiasm either.

"Engaged, bit sudden isn't it?"

"Yes daddy, it is but a woman just knows."

"Who is he? Anyone we might know? From round here is he?"

His name is William and he has the most soulful grey blue eyes daddy. You can see how he must have suffered in his early life. He doesn't want to talk about it. He says that he will one day when the memories have become a little less painful to remember. Some of the things he has had to go through would upset me if he told me now and he doesn't want to do that. He loves me too much. He is so clever. We enjoy the same books, and he has lots and lots of new ideas about the business. He said that we should branch out into second-hand cars, but none that were hooky or ringers. I never even heard of such a make. And car hire, with or without a driver. He knows lots of people in the trade, and scores of drivers looking for work who just need a chance to show what they can do."

"Yes, yes, but..."

"Not only that, but he can turn his hand to just about anything, he even wrote a book at one time but it was never published. Oh daddy, and you girls too, are just going to love my Billy. He has such a fund of funny stories about the goings on where he used to be, bent nails or crooked screws or something like that. He never did explain, but he fixed Aunty Maggie's Morris Minor and a leaking tap in her kitchen, and soon she was eating out of his hand and you know what an old sourpuss she can be at times."

"Don't I just."

"Her knight in shining armour she calls him."

"Well if that crabby old scarecrow has taken to him it will be a first. Do you know she didn't want your mother to marry me? Sour old cow."

"What does he do then, this wonder of all the virtues? Professional man? Not another mechanic or a plumber is he?"

"He is what you might call an entrepreneur. He has had his fingers into all sorts of businesses in the past. He even exported container loads of kippers to Africa once, how exciting. High risk-reward ventures he called some of them, and do you know I expect that the rascal has sailed a bit close to the wind sometimes, but he says that all the great business leaders do that from time to time, but that was when he was much younger. It's all water under the bridge now, daddy. He has turned over a new leaf. I believe it was just because he had never found the right woman before. God bless him because he has now. I do so want you to like him daddy."

She gave a deep sigh, which effectively ended the interrogation.

"Suppose I had better meet him, if he wants to ask for your hand."

"You will very soon. He just had a few bits of business to attend to first. I think that's his car I hear pulling onto the drive now. I gave him his own key."

The affianced, freshly groomed and shaven, sporting a crisp white shirt and regimental tie, entered the kitchen.

"Here you are darling, I would like you to meet my father."

The look on the paternal face was far beyond my poor ability to describe in mere words, but you may construct an inference from the way his cup danced in its saucer spilling half of its contents while the teaspoon, taking leave from its proper place, took aerial flight to hide under the kitchen table.

"What ho! Mr Soaper! Now, would you like me to call you Stanley, or perhaps you might prefer it if I was to call you dad?"